MURDER ON A SNOWY EVENING

A CAT LATIMER MYSTERY

LYNN CAHOON

CAT LATIMER COZY MYSTERIES

Murder on a Snowy Evening
Cat Latimer Mystery #9
Lynn Cahoon

DEDICATION

To my brother-in-law, Jim Gowin. Thanks for being the best role model for a life partner that a girl could have.

CHAPTER

ONE

January in Aspen Hills, Colorado is icy cold, snowy white, and filled with resolutions. A new semester at Covington College just started and the excitement for learning new things is overflowing from campus to the community. Especially at Cat Latimer's annual Reunion Writers Retreat and New Year's Goals and Plans for the Rest of Us. Seth Howard, Cat's boyfriend and live-in handyman had finished remodeling the new wing just before Christmas and just in time to finalize the event. Shauna Mary Clodagh, baker extraordinaire and Cat's partner in the retreats had sent the final confirmation for the eight participants in late November in the hope that Seth would come through and finish the west wing. At worst, Cat had assumed that they'd need to put the three extra writers up on the third floor.

Cat sat at the kitchen table looking at the week's schedule. It was busy, that was for sure. But the three 'reunion' writers were all friends of the retreat and were their guinea pigs for the next double retreat scheduled in March. Having this larger retreat quarterly at first, should prove the concept and not wear everyone out before they could evaluate the system. At least that was the plan

"You've gone over that schedule for the last three days. I'm making the airport run tomorrow. It's too late to add another speaker or event." Seth pulled the notebook away from Cat and nodded to her plate. "Eat. You always worry too much at the beginning of a retreat."

Cat picked up her fork and pushed around the homemade mac and cheese that Shauna had baked to go with the grilled salmon. "I hate change. I'm not sure if I realized how much until we started this retreat. Now I'm writing a new series *and* changing up the retreat. My change comfort meter is redlining."

Seth smiled at her. "It's fine. It's a soft opening for the reunion guests. We'll work out the bugs and prepare for March's opening. It's like Doctor Hollis says, you can't make an omelet without breaking some eggs."

Cat nodded and tried not to grit her teeth. She was getting tired of Doctor Kristin Hollis and her quaint little sayings and how she always sided with Seth during a fight. If Cat didn't know better, she'd say their relationship counselor had a bit of a crush on Cat's on again, off again, fiancé.

Shauna jumped into the conversation before Cat could react. She knew how Doctor Hollis grated on Cat's nerves. Bringing the woman into the conversation was probably not a good thing when Cat was already anxious. "Anyway, all Southern charm advice aside, Seth's right about the advantage of a soft opening. And we have three amazing people to test it out. Linda Cook, Deek Kerr, and Andi Grammy. If that isn't a group filled with positivity, I don't know one."

"We should also get valid suggestions from them," Cat added. She didn't need people who would just tell her the good things. She needed to know what didn't work. She took another bite of the mac and cheese. "I thought Uncle Pete was joining us for dinner. He's always so excited to give us the information from the background checks."

"Oh, I didn't tell you. Shirley showed up this afternoon for a surprise visit." Shauna broke off a bit of the fresh rolls she'd made for tonight's dinner and tomorrow's soup supper for the writers. "He says he'll drop the background checks off tomorrow, but not to worry."

Cat shook her head. "They're writers, I never worry."

Seth chuckled. "And that's one of the reasons your uncle insists on doing the background checks. At least we talked him out of doing the ones on the returning guests. That should save you some money."

Covington College hadn't killed their contract with Cat's writers' retreat last fall, but they had started charging a fee for the library use. One that Miss Applebome, the librarian, was thrilled to get each month as it paid for additional materials to the stacks. Without her having to get approval from the administration on what books to purchase.

Cat had put the clause in to win favor with the older librarian after hearing her complain about the hoops she had to go through on certain types of books. Censorship shouldn't be an issue in a college library. At least that was one topic Cat and Miss Applebome saw eye to eye on. Okay, maybe it was the only topic they agreed on.

Cat stood and refilled her coffee cup. She wasn't going to sleep much tonight anyway with the writers coming tomorrow. "I'm not sure we have enough activities for the reunion group. Especially with both of the groups focusing on setting their writing goals for the next year or so"

"If the writers want more, they'll tell us." Shauna set her fork down. "But I was wondering if we should group the returnees into genre groups. Like at least fiction and non-fiction. Linda's writing a memoir about her late husband. Andi's working on a novel. And so is Deek. This time it will be fine since the other group is all non-fiction writers."

"And there's two biography writers in that group, right?" Seth asked. "I think I might set in on the goal-setting session. Now that the house is almost finished, I need to get back to building my business as a community handyman. Having a master plan might help."

"Just remember you're still recovering with your leg. Please don't over-plan this year. The doctor said it might be two years before you're back to full strength." Cat worried about how much Seth was already doing. He'd been shot on a mission last summer with his mercenary contract crew and had just stopped using a cane to support his leg. Now he was back home but not in the same shape as when he'd left. Besides, the man never slowed down. Even when it was for his own good.

"Yes, mother." Seth met Cat's gaze and winked. "All I'm saying is it's not a bad idea to set some goals for the new year for my business and personally. I'm sure you've got some already percolating."

Shauna giggled. "I'd be surprised if Cat didn't have every month already worked out by now. If not laminated and hung over her desk."

"You two realize that I work on contracts. If I have a book due the end of this month, I started it last year." Cat finished her dinner and took her plate to the sink where she rinsed it and put it in the dishwasher. "Although I would love to have a three or five-year plan. I don't want to get stuck in a rut."

"I'm planning out the next two years at least with the cookbooks. I only have one more on my contract and who knows if they'll renew it. So it's time to go back to the basics and brainstorm out a few new ideas." Shauna put her dish in the sink. "We've talked about the reunion group, do you want to chat about the other writers?"

"Please," Seth stood and cleared his plate and took some of the other things off the table. "I like knowing a bit about them so the four-hour drive back here from the Denver airport isn't quiet and uncomfortable."

Shauna wiped the table off with a damp cloth and then grabbed her notebook. Seth had a notebook he'd brought to dinner as well.

Cat hadn't been as prepared for this discussion. She'd thought they'd talk tomorrow morning, so she grabbed a new notebook from Shauna's stash in the office desk. And a new pen. Shauna was always buying new pens and this one looked expensive.

"Okay, we have four writers, three are working on self-help and goal-setting books. One on habits, that's Wilder Russ. Felix Phillips says his book is on building systems for your goals. And then Piper Caldwell, she's focused on setting goals correctly for success. They're all looking forward to Professor Presley's talk on Tuesday. Jewel Doan is working on a biography of a contemporary writer. That's all she'd tell me. But she should have a lot in common with Linda Cook and the Covington Student, Ryan Garett. He writes about local authors and their development. I'm sure Tom Cook will be mentioned in his book. Ryan wants a list of all the writers who have come through our program. Cat, before I gave it to him, I wanted to clear it with you first."

Cat looked up from her notebook as she considered the question. "I don't know. Are we assuring people that their stay here is private? Maybe we can ask the people who have been published if they don't mind us releasing their information to Ryan. Let me chat with him and see what he specifically needs for his project. I'm sure he doesn't want everyone."

"Especially all those who haven't moved past just writing. If I was still figuring out who I was going to be as an author, I'm not sure I'd want my name released. Besides, I wouldn't have time to chat with some student, work a day job, and write. Most of your writers are still working for a living." Seth tapped his pen on the notebook. "Is that it? I need to let Sam out soon."

"That's it." Shauna handed him a list of everyone's flight information. "You should be able to do this in one trip if you buy Wilder lunch while you wait for the other authors to arrive."

"Sounds like a plan. And I'll take a book, just in case they aren't chatty while we wait. Can someone check on Sam and let him out a couple of times while I'm gone?" Seth stood and tucked his planner under his arm.

Shauna smiled and tapped her planner. "Already on my list for tomorrow. If the weather cooperates, we'll go for a short walk. Do you have snow booties for him?"

Seth shook his head. "Sam hates them. Just don't keep him out long in the cold."

Cat waited until Seth had left the kitchen and she'd heard the door to the west wing open and close. Then she turned to Shauna. "He doesn't look tired to you, does he?"

"Cat, you can't keep him from working. Seth knows when he needs to slow down. But I take it from your look when Seth mentioned your therapist that your counseling sessions aren't going well. What's going on?" Shauna stood and filled the tea kettle, then settled it on the stove to heat. "We probably need to chat now since next week's going to be a madhouse with three more guests than usual."

"I don't know. I think it's going okay." Cat tucked her pen onto the notebook, then leaned back. "He says all the right things. The counselor thinks we're making great progress, but I guess I'm still scared that when he does heal up, he'll jump at the first chance he has to go back to the contract work. He says he's done, but he's said that before."

"Has he told you why he went last time?" Shauna set their cups up with a cinnamon apple spice tea they'd just found at a local Christmas bazaar.

"Vaguely. He said he felt like his team needed him." Cat met Shauna's gaze. "But what about us? We need him here for the retreat. I need him here."

"You need to tell him that and see how he reacts. Guys like being all macho and such, but they also need to know they are appreciated. Seth does a lot around here which we pay him for, but he's not just an employee. He's the first person to greet the writers as they come to town. He's the last person to talk to them. He's a big part of the retreat, just like you are as the resident author and I take care of their every need so they can write."

"You're the food goddess," Cat smiled as she thought about Seth's role in the retreat. "You're right. He's gone from just fixing the house to being part of the retreat itself. I know he started working the full retreat week due to some issues with guests, but he's more than just staff now. If he wasn't here, the retreat wouldn't be as relaxing for the guests."

"Maybe we need a retreat staff party or our own retreat to get us out of town for a few days this winter to relax. I could check the budget and see what we can afford." Shauna filled the cups with steaming water and then brought the tea over to the table and sat down. "I've always wanted to go spend a week on a tropical beach."

"Let's bring Seth into the conversation. I'm sure he's got some ideas on where we should go." Cat dunked her teabag into the water and closed her eyes when the cinnamon smell surrounded her. "But let's not do a cruise. I want to go and then relax for a week. Not travel all the time."

"You haven't been on the right cruises. Kevin and I went to Greece a few years ago. It was magical." Shauna smiled but the emotion didn't hit her eyes.

"You still miss him?" Cat wondered if she was poking at a wound. Kevin had been killed before he and Shauna had gotten married, but she'd loved him.

"I do. Dante's trying to get my mind on other things, but he comes with a lot of baggage that I'm not sure I'm ready to take on." Shauna looked at Cat. "And I don't think he would walk away from the baggage. Not for me. Maybe for someone else if she asked."

Cat shook her head. "Don't go there. There's nothing between Dante and me. If that's holding you back, don't let it."

Shauna laughed. "Cat, you know that his feelings for you aren't even the biggest issue we have between us. We're having fun right now and that's probably all it's going to be. Let's get back to this vacation. Do you think we have room to plan for January, even though we are running the retreat a week later than usual?"

THE NEXT MORNING, Cat woke with a plan. She had a book due the first of March, but if she focused this week and got words in the morning, and participated in all the word sprint times, she could take the week off for their staff retreat without writing on the beach. She brushed her hair as she looked at the woman in the mirror. "Now we just need to get Seth on board."

Today was a writing day for her even though it was a weekend. Seth would go get the writers, then they'd have soup with everyone for dinner. Tomorrow, the entire group would go snowshoeing. Shauna had already bailed on the activity using the excuse that she was making the group dinner for Sunday night. Homemade individual chicken pot pies with a green salad. And she was making chili and cornbread and taking it out to their halfway spot for lunch. She'd drive to the mountain-top park and set up the meal. Then if anyone was worn out after going that far, she'd take them back to the house. Cat hoped she could talk Seth into only doing half the snowshoeing adventure, but she hadn't brought it up yet. She'd fight that battle later.

She got dressed in sweats and a Covington College sweatshirt and went downstairs for coffee. And maybe something sweet.

When she arrived in the kitchen, Seth was already eating breakfast and Cat's uncle was at the table with a plate of eggs, ham, and breakfast potatoes in front of him. "Hey guys, I didn't see the invite to the breakfast meeting on my calendar."

"I was dropping off the background checks for your records. So far, your writer group is a picture of normalcy. Not a robbery or attempted murder charge among them." Uncle Pete pointed his fork at Seth. "This one was bragging about how amazing Shauna's eggs were, so I had to check them out."

Shauna laughed as she set a plate in front of an empty chair. "Sit down, Cat. I know you just came for coffee, but the morning has turned into a family meal."

"Fine, but only because I want to hear about Shirley being here. I can't believe she just dropped in. Especially since you two just spent New Year's Eve together in Alaska." Cat poured herself a cup of coffee and sat down at the table. "Where is she? I thought maybe you'd bring her with you."

"She had something to do in Denver. That woman holds her cards close to her chest. I respect that about her. I do the same, so maybe it's our work in law enforcement that's allowed us to compartmentalize things." He took a bite of breakfast potatoes. "On the other hand, you three work and live together. I don't see how you can have any secrets."

"If you're talking about me dating Dante, Cat and Seth already know." Shauna sat at the table with her own plate. "And it's not serious so there's no tea to spill about that."

"Just be careful," Uncle Pete met her gaze. "I don't want anyone to think that you might be a good leverage point for Mr. Cornelio. Neither he nor you are part of the college, so your Covington protection is a little suspect."

Cat shook her head. "Shauna is a Covington College contractor and Dante is the family representative for the college. They both should be protected."

"You have a lot of faith in people who use murder as a business tactic." Uncle Pete held up his hand. "I'm not going to fight this battle anymore. I just want Shauna to be careful."

"I agree with Pete. Dante's dangerous. Even if he comes across as innocent. You're dealing with a scorpion. Violence is in his nature." Seth cleaned his plate, then stood and took it to the counter. "I need to check on Sam. Nice to see you, Pete."

As he left the room, Cat's gaze followed him. "Shauna, you can't listen to them."

Shauna smiled. "I know who Dante Cornelio is and what he's capable of doing. I also know he's kind, compassionate, and fun to be around. I'm going to date who I want to and respectfully, Pete, you and Seth can stay out of it."

Cat laughed as she focused on eating. "And that's that."

Uncle Pete refilled his coffee cup. "I'm not sure what I did in a previous life to be cursed with having to care about so many strong women in this life."

"Cursed is such a strong word," Shauna squeezed Pete's hand. "I'd use the word, blessed. It makes us feel better."

CHAPTER

TWO

Cat finally pulled herself out of her office and away from the writing at four so she could grab a shower and change into real clothes before greeting the writers. Of course, maybe seeing her with her hair in a clip and her sweatshirt with food and coffee stains would have been a more realistic picture of her 'author' life. She just wasn't ready to totally pull back the curtain, yet.

It was good to have a fantasy of what real authors did during the day. And what they looked like. On the other hand, she loved her life now a lot more than when she was dressing to be in front of a classroom of students or in a faculty meeting. She didn't have to leave the house if she didn't want to, and she could still earn a paycheck. Even if that paycheck came in lump sums and she was unable to predict what amount she would be paid. Unless it was her advance.

She wondered if she needed to add a piece about the money part of being an author. She could do it for the advanced class. That way, she wouldn't burst their excitement bubble over someday giving up the day job. It was possible, but full-time authors dealt with how to stretch an advance, how to find health insurance, and other fun subjects you didn't think of when you worked for 'the man'. Like putting money away into a retirement fund.

Cat would probably write until she stopped making full sentences that made sense, but it would be nice to be able to plan for more than a week off. She grabbed the notebook she always kept in her bedroom and wrote down a note on developing a session on the *Financial Fate of a Full-Time Author – Fact and Fiction.* She'd pull something together for Wednesday's retreat group and then expand it for the next reunion session.

As she made her way downstairs, she put the ripped-out page on her desk in her office to remind her to block out some planning time. Then she turned out the light. The door had a Do NOT ENTER – PRIVATE sign on it to keep wandering writers from thinking it was available for their writing nook. Cat would share her house with strangers, but not her writing desk. She needed the privacy to help her craft her stories. The office was where Tori, the main character in her books lived. At least in Cat's mind.

When she got downstairs, the group was milling around the foyer where Shauna was getting them checked in. Cat was late. She threw an apologetic smile at Shauna and went to the next person in the line. He wore a lanyard around his neck with a nametag that read, Felix Phillips, Productivity Specialist. Cat held out her hand. "Mr. Phillips, so nice to meet you."

"I recognize you from your author picture, Cat Latimer. I read several of your books in preparation for coming here." He shook her hand, vigorously. "I see you took advantage of my nametag hack. I always wear one of these if I'm going to be around people I don't know. A lot of people don't want others to know who they are, but not me. How will you buy my future book if you don't remember my name and how it's spelled?"

"Well, that's a good point." Cat pointed to Shauna who had just finished handing Andi Grammy her room key. "Shauna will check you in with your credit card and a photo ID."

Felix frowned and held up his lanyard. "I don't have one in my pen name."

"Don't worry about it. It's only for our records and for payment. We'll call you Felix or any other name you want." Cat put a hand on his back and gently moved him toward Shauna. Felix was going to be a detail person. She turned and gave Andi a hug. "I'm so glad you are one of our test subjects for the reunion week."

"Are you kidding? I'm so excited to be back." Andi hugged her tightly. "I know I have my writer group in the real world, but this just seems like my writer persona's home. Besides, I missed Shauna's cooking. I dieted all last month, so I'd be prepared for this week."

Cat laughed and pointed her over to where Seth was standing. "I need to do that every month. You're going to be in the west wing so Seth will show you to your room."

"Seth! I haven't seen you in weeks." Andi lived in town so she'd come directly to the retreat.

Cat smiled as she turned to the next person in line. "I'm Cat Latimer. I'm so happy you could attend our retreat this week."

"Me, too. I'm Piper Caldwell" An older woman in jeans and a blazer looked around the foyer. "Your home is beautiful. I guess I've been in the corporate world too long. I was expecting a Holiday Inn and a conference room."

"We like to share our beautiful Victorian." Cat pointed to Seth who was helping Andi with her bag. "My fiancé, Seth Howard, did most of the restoration. This was one of the college's original faculty housings back in the day. The good news is that we brought it back from its frat house days without a whole lot of repair work. You'll be on the second floor of this wing, but you should visit the west wing where our reunion guests are staying. It's amazing."

"I'll definitely check it out. I've always been interested in old houses. My husband just laughs when I say we should buy one and fix it up. He has more modern tastes." Piper nodded to Shauna who was waving her over. "I'm up. I'm looking forward to snowshoeing tomorrow. We live in Florida so I'm excited about getting out in the snow."

Cat smiled as she went to the next guest. Snowshoeing didn't require the skills of downhill, but it was still physically demanding. Seth had offered to take the group out a second time on Thursday if anyone wanted to go again. She thought she'd be busy writing that day. Deek Kerr was next in line and his blond cornrows were tipped in purple for this visit. He dropped his bags and pulled her into a hug.

"It's so good to see you. And you and Seth are better, I see. Your auras are weaving colors together." He held her at arm's length as he studied the colors around her that only he could see. "Peach and blue, they make a beautiful mix."

"Good to see you again, Deek. How's South Cove?" Cat squeezed his arms, then stepped out of the hug. Deek had been on a recent retreat, and she'd taken a shine to the surfer dude gone author.

"The bookstore is flourishing and my boss is amazing. She said she really wants you to schedule a stop on the next tour. Of course, I'd be your contact for any author event." He puffed up his chest in an exaggerated motion. "I'm a man of many talents."

"And many words, Deek, come on over here and let Cat meet the next writer." Shauna waved him over as Piper made her way to the grand staircase to go up to her room.

"Shauna, you look lovely, as always. I'm going to have a red-headed beauty in my next book. Do you want to be a villain or a hero?" Deek grabbed his duffel bag and headed over to the registration desk.

A young man stepped in front of her, holding out his hand. "I'm Ryan Garett. I'm a Covington student. They said they were covering my costs this week?"

"You are correct. Shauna will get a copy of your student identification and an emergency contact and give you your room key." Cat took a breath before she asked the next question. She never knew what genre or specialty the Covington students would be studying.

In the background information the department had sent over on Ryan, it had just said general studies. "So what are you focusing on in your masters? Fiction or non-fiction?"

"Oh, I figured they would have said something. I'm working on my thesis on authors who have attended Covington and, specifically, your workshop. It's kind of a biography but with a lot of different people. Tom Cook attended the retreat, right? I mean, before he was murdered?" Ryan dropped his voice and looked around. "There's a rumor that his wife is going to be here as well."

"It's not a rumor, I'm here as one of the reunion guests." Linda Cook stood behind Ryan and waved at Cat. "Sorry, I was eavesdropping. I'll be glad to talk to you about my husband sometime this week. His legacy is very important to me and our family."

A woman behind her snorted. "His legacy. I don't think you're going to like my book where I expose your sainted husband for the lecherous man he was."

Linda turned toward the woman. "Excuse me?"

"You heard what I said. I'm Jewel Doan. Your husband and I were having an affair the last year of his life. And boy, did he tell me some things about the life of an author. He said he had women all across the country." Jewel's eyes narrowed as she looked at Ryan. "I'm not sure you'll want to include him in your thesis. Unless you don't care about an author's moral code."

"Look, I don't know what you're talking about. I'm sure you're confused. Tom and I were happy. He didn't cheat on me and most times, I went with him on his book tours. So whatever you're trying to sell, it's not going to work. Find some other celebrity to hook your star to." Linda nodded to Shauna. "I'm going to go check in now. I hope this is the last conversation we'll have. Ever."

Ryan looked at Cat. "I was next in line."

"Let's get Linda to her room. I'm sure she'll appreciate it. Just stand here and Shauna will help you as soon as possible." Cat took Jewel's arm and pulled her aside. "Look, I don't know what's going on or who's telling the truth, but we can't have scenes like this. Can you please leave Linda Cook alone? If not, I'll need to schedule you for a different month. I'll pay for your ticket home."

Jewel opened her mouth, threw a killer glance at Linda's back, then nodded. "I'm sorry. My flight was horrible and I have a wretched headache. It took an act of God for me to get this time off. I can't reschedule. I'll leave her alone. I don't need to interview her for my book. I already have most of it written. I just needed to experience Covington and Aspen Hills. And of course, where Tom was killed."

"You're sure you can avoid another blow-up like this?" Cat asked again as Linda Cook went over to where Seth was now waiting by the west wing entrance. Jewel nodded. "Okay, I'm going to hold you to your promise. I don't know you. Linda is a friend and has supported the retreat since Tom died. You have to know I'll side with her if there's another incident. I'm just being honest."

"It's fine. I'll be good. I promise." She pushed her long blonde hair back away from her face. "I'm not doing anything to risk the offer I have on the table for the book already. That kind of money is life-changing. I just need to get to my room and take something for this migraine."

Cat looked over and Shauna had already checked Ryan into his room. She pointed over to the registration desk. "Shauna can help you check in, then."

She took a breath before greeting the next and the last guest, Wilder Russ. She introduced herself. "I'm sorry about that little blowup. Typically, our writer retreats are pretty boring."

"Oh, I've heard differently." Wilder shook her hand, a big grin on his face. "You have to know you're called the murder retreat on the internet. There's a whole group of writers who post about their experiences here at the retreat. The ones where you don't have a murder have guests who are a little sad they didn't get the full treatment. I mean, I know it's bad for someone to die, but it does spice up the writers' retreat, right?"

Shauna had invited everyone back to the dining room for soup and bread so when dinner was served, Cat made herself available in the dining room. She brought the last basket of rolls out and set them on the buffet. "Shauna, the food looks amazing. I'm sure they'll love it."

"Jewel has already asked if someone can bring up a bowl to her room. She's really fighting that migraine. My cousin has migraines, and they can wipe her out for a week." Shauna glanced around the room, making sure everything was in place.

"Make sure she knows we don't usually do room service. I'd hate for her to come to expect this." Cat didn't know if Tom Cook had been unfaithful to Linda, but as she'd told Jewel, Linda was a friend. "I should have had her reschedule. This is going to be tense."

Wilder and a few others came into the room and formed a line by the buffet. Shauna and Cat moved to be near the doorway. Shauna leaned closer. "She'll be fine. Sometimes you just have to say something and get it out there. I think a long travel day and the headache has put Jewel in a bad mood. She'll be better tomorrow. I'd bet money on it."

"Yeah, but there's still the claim she was sleeping with Tom Cook." Cat smiled as more of the writers came into the dining room. "There are rumors about the bigger writer conventions being a place to well, hook up. I didn't see it at the paranormal conferences I attended, but I've heard stories."

"You'll have to tell me some, later. I'm taking a tray up to Jewel and then eating in the kitchen. I've got a book calling my name." Shauna picked up an already empty breadbasket to take back to the kitchen. "Are you eating with them?"

"Yes, I'll be the extrovert author for the meal. Luckily, snowshoeing isn't a very chatty excursion, or I'd be done for the week by Sunday night." Cat smiled and went to the end of the line where Linda Cook was standing and looking around, probably for Jewel. "Hey Linda, mind if I sit by you?"

She blew out her breath. "That would be perfect. I get Tom's fans coming up to me all the time wanting to talk about him but something like what she claimed. It kind of shocked me. I'm sorry if I made a scene."

"Linda, if someone threw something like that in my face about Seth, I would have slapped her. Or knocked her over." Cat picked up a bowl and went straight to the chicken noodle. Shauna had given them four choices – a veggie chili, a creamy potato with all the fixings to make loaded potato soup, a beef stew, and chicken soup with homemade noodles. All of the soups were homemade. It was part of a Comfort Foods Cookbook Shauna had been working on for the last couple of months.

"Well, I promise to be more discreet when she comes at me again." Linda filled her bowl with the potato soup. "I didn't think I was hungry until I smelled the freshly baked bread. Shauna is amazing in the kitchen."

"Yes, she is. But listen, if Jewel does this again, just let me know. I'll send her packing." Cat pointed to the bacon bits. "Are you making it loaded?"

There were talks about doing a writing sprint after dinner, but Cat could see that most of them weren't really up to writing. The new guests were tired after their long flight. Deek, who'd come in from California looked over at Andi who still lived in Aspen Hills. "There's an alcove on our floor in the west wing. Do you want to meet there in a few minutes and write for a sprint or two?"

"Sounds like the best way to open up this January retreat." Andi looked over at Linda and Cat. "Linda, you're our other 'reunion' guest. If you want to join us, you're more than welcome."

"I'm heading to my room to soak in that extremely large claw foot tub I saw in my bathroom." Linda stood as she said goodnight. "I'll see you all tomorrow for our snowshoeing adventure."

Piper stood as well. "I'm not saying I can get very far, but I'll give it the college try. Especially since we're in a college town. Get it?"

The others groaned at her attempt at humor.

"Whatever. By the end of the week, I'll have you laughing at my dad jokes just to keep me from telling another one." Piper grabbed a couple of peanut butter cookies. She turned back to meet Cat's gaze. "Thanks for the basket in our room and water. This is like being in a fancy hotel."

"There's a small fridge near your bookshelf too." Deek went over to get more chili. "That's an upgrade."

Cat laughed. "For the west wing, yes. The second floor has to deal with an ice bucket. We have a machine by the stairs in a small room."

"The west wing residents have their own fridges?" Felix grinned. "One more reason for me to come back as an alumnus."

Cat hid a yawn behind her hand. "We'll be upgrading the second floor soon. It's on our wish list for this year."

"Well, I wish you the best on that, but I'm still coming back. Especially if I get as much work done here as I'm planning. Being away from my wife and kids has just decreased my chore list down to nothing for the week. I should have plenty of time to write." Felix grabbed a cookie and took a bite.

"Dude, you just jinxed yourself. Never assume you're going to get more done because sometimes, things happen." Deek slapped Felix's back as he walked back to sit down with his chili. "Besides, you haven't even made your weekly goal list. Be optimistic but realistic. Right Cat?"

"And Deek has just given you your first assignment for the retreat. By Monday at five, I want your weekly goal plan in the box on the registration desk. The forms are already there and you can pick yours up any time before Monday noon." Cat stood. "And with that, I'm saying goodnight. The doors lock at ten, but you all have a code to get back in. If you're really stuck, there's a buzzer that will sound in Seth's room. He'll let you in. But he won't be happy about it."

Cat said her goodnights and headed to the kitchen with a tray of dirty dishes. She walked in and set them on the counter. Shauna was reading at the table and looked up when she came in. "I think I'm heading to bed."

"You didn't have to bring those in. I'll clean up the dining room before I turn in." Shauna pushed a plate of cookies toward Cat. "Try one of those. It's a new recipe."

Cat sank into a chair and took a cookie. "I really hope this retreat goes well. I have a bad feeling about it."

"Well, Jewel was mortified she verbally attacked Mrs. Cook. She told me she never even planned on telling her about the affair." Shauna set her book down after tucking in a bookmark.

"Do you think she's telling the truth?" Cat asked as she broke the cookie in half. "I didn't know Tom Cook well, but an affair?"

"She thinks she is. Maybe it was someone else she met who looked like Tom. I don't know. I just know she looked wounded when I took up her dinner." Shauna leaned back in her chair. "We've never had this situation before."

Cat took another cookie. "I guess Uncle Pete was right, sometimes people are trouble. But this is one problem a background check wouldn't have found."

THREE

S nowshoeing on the agenda started at ten on Sunday morning. Shauna didn't want to get the writers up too early. The first stop was the local outdoor rental store to get everyone bundled into snowsuits and shoes. Cat had made an appointment, so the store knew they were coming. Shauna had asked everyone for their clothing and shoe sizes so that the rental place would have their outfits ready. Cat and Seth had their own, but Seth wasn't going to be their guide on this trip. Normally, he would but he'd woke with pain in his leg so he was going to drive them out to the trailhead where he'd leave them with a hired guide. Then he'd bring lunch to the group rather than Shauna at the midpoint where they'd turn around.

Linda pulled Cat aside as they were getting on the bus. "I'm not going with you this morning. I need to check on our cabin so I'll be hiking in to make sure it's okay. I should be back by evening, but if I'm not, here's the address and travel directions. I should have come last fall, but I didn't want to deal with it. Tom used the cabin for writing when he was on deadline, and I haven't been there since he died."

"That's been years." Cat didn't want to think about what the cabin might actually look like. "Maybe you shouldn't go alone. Do you want me to go with you?"

"No, I'm fine. I've had Seth go up and check the cabin twice a year, but with him down with his leg, I didn't feel right asking him to check it out this year. Anyway, the worst that could happen is I'll find too many memories." She smiled at Cat. "Don't worry, you look like I'm hiking the Appalachian trail by myself or going up Mount Everest. It's not a bad walk from the trailhead and I have Shauna's snowshoes and gear. She even packed me some food and a thermos of hot chocolate."

"Okay, but if you run into trouble, don't go off the trail. People get lost in the mountains all the time because they decide to take a shortcut." No matter what Linda said, Cat *was* worried. She'd lived in the mountains long enough to know that going off on your own wasn't always smart. When it worked, it was fine, but when it didn't, well, people died. "Linda, why don't you come with us today and I'll go with you to the cabin tomorrow?"

Linda wasn't listening. Jewel had come out of the dining room and was chatting with Ryan. She turned back to Cat, a grimace on her face. "Look, I've got to go. My car's outside warming up."

Cat watched as Linda took off out the front door to avoid Jewel. No matter what she'd said about being okay, clearly, she wasn't comfortable with the other woman around. After Linda drove off, she went into the kitchen to check in with Shauna. "So you knew about Linda's field trip?"

"Yes, and I tried to talk her out of it. I called Shirley and asked if she wouldn't mind going with her and she agreed. Now I just need to tell Linda that Shirley's coming." Shauna pulled a bunch of oversized cookies out of the oven.

"Too late, Linda just took off. I'm not sure her going alone is a good idea." Cat handed Shauna the information that Linda had left with her. "Maybe Shirley could hike up this afternoon and meet her on the way out."

"I'll call her and let her know the change of plans. I'm sure Linda will be fine getting there, but if she stays too long in the cabin, she might not realize that she's going to lose the light as early as we do in the winter." Shauna pulled off the hot pads and grabbed the phone, texting Shirley the updated information. "I've already noticed an increase in problems with just adding three people into our retreat group. I'm not sure how many more we should consider adding."

Cat nodded. "I didn't realize the increase in personal dynamics issues would be this bad. I mean, how do you screen for possible affairs and secret mistresses?"

"Do you believe Jewel?" Shauna took the cookies off the sheet to cool on a wire rack.

"I don't know. She seems genuine. When I told her to cool her jets, she was apologetic and worried about keeping her spot in the retreat. I guess she wants the background information for her book." Cat refilled her coffee cup. "I'm not sure she'd go to this much trouble if she was making up the affair."

"Yeah, that's what's bothering me too." Shauna started tucking cooled cookies into plastic bags for the trip. "Why spend the money on a retreat here to find out more about the subject if you're just making up your relationship with him? I'd find a warm destination where I knew he'd attended a conference and go there."

Cat picked up a cookie on the serving platter that was going out to the dining room and broke it in half. "That fact doesn't make sense. I wonder if Uncle Pete's background check had anything on Jewel. Can you look while we're gone? If the situation gets much more tense, I'm going to have to ask one of them to leave. And I don't think it should be Linda."

Shauna counted the filled bags and then put them into a carrying case. "At least by bringing them in early, we might clear up any of these issues before the hard work of the retreat starts."

Cat laughed as she picked up the box. "I take it this is for the trip?"

"Yes, I have a box of water bottles and coffee thermos, as well already by the front door. They can fill their thermos with what they want and the water bottles will be in the van for them to take when you guys get to the trail." She nodded to the box. "There's a cookie bag, a savory bag, and a trail mix bag in there for everyone. I'll bring more snacks and drinks with lunch. Or Seth will. Or maybe both of us will come."

Cat went out to the foyer where everyone was gathering. She explained how the day was going to be structured, then warned everyone to make sure they stayed together on the mountain. "We don't want anyone to get lost."

Felix chuckled. "Don't you worry about me, I'm not letting any of you out of my sight. I've seen the disaster movies. I don't want to be the first man down."

"You don't have a prison for the criminally insane nearby, do you?" Wilder asked.

"Dude, you're scaring the women." Deek laughed and then added. "Along with me. I'm sure if there was an escaped convict or serial killer, Cat would be the first to know."

"I think my uncle would pick up all of us and have us do a sleep-over at the jail until the guy was found. He's a little protective." Cat grabbed her snowsuit and struggled into her snow jacket.

"I'll agree with Cat. You should have seen the guy when Cat and I were dating in high school. I was afraid to adjust her coat in case he thought I was touching her, inappropriately." Seth grabbed the box of water bottles. "Did everyone get a thermos and fill it with their favorite brew? No alcohol I'm afraid until we get back. Your guide doesn't need to be wrangling drunk snowshoers off the trail."

"Dude, I didn't think you were going with us," Deek slapped Seth on the back. "I'm stoked."

"Don't be too excited, Deek. I'm dropping you off, feeding you lunch, then picking you back up. Make sure you get some pictures so you can show them to me at dinner. I haven't been on that trail all year. I'm getting a little twitchy being stuck on the sidelines." Deek glanced at his watch. "We're leaving in five minutes. Go get your drinks and hit the bathroom because I'm not stopping again until we hit the rental shop."

"Yes, Dad," Felix and Wilder said in unison. Then they slapped their hands in a high five.

As people hurried to get ready to leave, Cat met Seth's gaze. "I really wish you were coming."

"With that group, I bet you do. They seem more social than I'd expect from data nerds." Seth nodded to the van. "I need to get these water's stored. Bring the box of treats too."

When they got to the trailhead, the excited chatter had slowed as the forest got deeper and darker. And the snow drifts taller.

"Maybe this isn't a good idea." Piper glanced at the window. "It's not going to snow today, right?"

"We'll be fine. No snow in the forecast and we have a clear trail to follow. If we think it's an issue when Seth brings up lunch, we'll cut it short then." Hank Rogers, the guide for the day, stood in the van. "You're in good hands. I've done this hike in my sleep."

"Uphill both ways and in five feet of snow," Seth added, a smile on his face. "Literally."

'Funny guy," Cat climbed out of the van and stretched before slipping on her snowsuit. She went to the back grabbed treat bags and tucked them away in the many pockets in her suit. Then she put a water bottle on the strap that circled her waist. She pulled down her beanie over her ears and looked around. She called out, "There's treats and water for you back here."

Seth stood by her as the group got ready. "Okay, nine of you are going in. I expect to see nine for lunch. So watch out for each other."

Deek saluted Seth. "Yes, sir. I didn't realize snowshoeing was a team sport."

"Anything you do out here in the wilderness should be a team sport. Going out by yourself in winter or any time of year is just stupid." Hank adjusted his pack and looked at the others gathered around him. "Let's go slay this."

Seth gave Cat a kiss and closed up the van. "I'll see you at one thirty."

"Sounds good." Cat was already thinking about Linda going to her cabin alone. Maybe she should have insisted, but she didn't want to look like she didn't believe in the woman. She nodded to Seth as she fell in line. Shirley would catch up with Linda.

Deek had taken the role of last in their line, so he smiled at her. "You always make these retreats exciting. I don't get to do a lot of snowshoeing on the coast."

"Yeah, but you get to play in the ocean with the sharks and fish." They were already past where she could have seen Seth. The woods had turned silent around them, and the outside world seemed to disappear behind them.

Cat focused on the walk. Snowshoeing was physical and she'd been ignoring her runs lately. Piper and Jewel were chatting ahead of her.

"I'd never do anything like this at home," Piper admitted. "Although I did want to try out cross-country skiing. I have a ski resort about thirty minutes away from my house. What about you? Have you been to Colorado before?"

"I had a layover in Denver once." Jewel was looking around. "I thought there would be more cabins and such around us."

"I think they're tucked away. I heard Seth say that this trail is on the edge of a national forest. I guess once you get inside one, people aren't allowed to build or buy land. It's all set aside for public use." Piper took in a deep breath of fresh air. "I was totally tired of Christmas before I left home, but this looks like we're walking through a Christmas card."

"Yeah, I guess." Jewel didn't seem as entranced as Piper was with the scenery.

Cat was falling behind, and the women's conversation was getting harder to listen to. She wouldn't say she was eavesdropping but listening to them helped her pass the time. And it gave her vital information to make the writers' retreat more personal.

She watched as Jewel took off and left Piper as she pointed out an owl in the tree. She hurried to try to catch up with the now-alone Piper. "Hey, was that an owl?"

Piper grinned as she took out her phone and showed Cat the picture. "I guess Jewel isn't into wildlife. I was chatting with her as I took the picture, then I turned around and I was alone. I was hoping to make a friend, but Linda didn't come today and well I seemed to have run Jewel off."

"I'm sure it wasn't personal." Cat handed Piper back the phone. "Linda had to go and check out the cabin she owns near here. I'm sure you'll have a lot of time to make a connection this week."

"Ladies, we're lagging behind and Hank asked me to make sure we don't get out of sight of the rest of the group." Deek came up to Cat's right side. "Everything okay?"

"We're fine. Just looking at Piper's owl." Cat nodded to Piper. "Are you ready?"

They started walking and Cat thought about Jewel. Would she be able to make friends with the group at all? Piper had been more than open to the idea, but Jewel had left her in the dust, so to speak. Cat might need to ask the woman to leave after all.

When they got to the meeting spot for lunch, Jewel wasn't with them. Cat pulled Hank aside as Shauna and Seth set up lunch as the writers fell into place on the picnic tables. "Where's Jewel?"

"The other woman?" Hank glanced at Piper who was chatting with Deek. "She asked if I knew a shortcut back to Harris Hollow. She said she had a friend with a cabin there. The trail's all downhill and marked well, so I gave her a map. She said she'd cleared the detour with you."

"No, she hadn't. She lives in New Jersey. How can she have a friend here?" Hank was from Denver and went to school at Covington. This outdoor tour guide job was just until he finished his schooling and got into law school. She'd had to listen to his self-proclaimed bio as the writers got their snowsuits at the rental company. "So she said she was going to Harris Hollow? Did she mention the friend's name?"

Hank shook his head. "Look, if I'd known she wasn't a native, I wouldn't have let her go. Andi was talking with her, and I know Andi. I just thought she must live here."

And this was another reason Seth would have been a much better guide. He actually thought before he acted. "Just make sure none of the other writers take off on our way back, okay?"

"Definitely. Is there food for me too?" Hank pointed to the bags on the table.

Cat nodded. "Of course. I need to go talk to Seth and Shauna."

She followed Hank to the food table and grabbed a sandwich. She went over to where Seth and Shauna were standing watching the sky. "What's going on?"

"It looks like a storm might be coming in. The weather says it should hold off until you get back to the trailhead. Do you need me to take anyone back to the house?" Seth took a bite of his sandwich.

"You might ask Piper. But there's a problem. Jewel took off on a trail down to Harris Hollow. Hank gave her a map and everything." She glared at Hank's back. "He's an idiot. He thought she was a local and Andi's friend."

"So after that whole talk about safety first he gave, he let someone go off on her own?" Seth pulled his trail map out of his coat pocket. "I'll stop at the trailhead and hike the trail for a bit to see if I can find her."

Cat watched as he rubbed his wounded leg. "Can you just check out the trailhead? Unless her friend is a skier, no one's going to be at a remote cabin this time of year. I don't think you should go looking. She could be hooking up with someone she knows."

"Your writers are hard to keep track of." Seth finished his sandwich. "Don't worry about it. The good news is she's heading down the mountain toward the Forest Service office so she should be able to make a call from there. Even if they've already left, they leave their Wi-Fi going just in case someone needs help. At least we know she has a map."

"Hank's an idiot. He never should have let her go off on her own." Cat watched as Deek stood up and scanned the area. "And now she's been missed. I don't care if she wanted to go off on her own, but now, she's affecting other writers on the retreat. I bet you Deek's already noticed she's missing."

"He's like an old mother hen watching her chicks. He befriended Stephen the last time he was here. And you know what a mess that guy was at the time." Shauna added. "Look, go tell Deek but then you eat. If you're going down with them, you need to eat."

"True. I'm feeling the adventure today." Cat went over and grabbed a thermos of soup and a cookie. Then she went and sat next to Deek.

"Cat, I think Jewel's missing," Deek sat next to her and lowered his voice. "I don't want to worry anyone."

"She went her own way a few miles back. Hank sent her down to a residential area to try to find a friend's cabin."

"He let her go alone. Is he insane?" Deek glared at the guide, but since Hank was focused on eating the gesture was lost on him.

"Possibly. Look, Seth's going to check out the trail he sent her on when he goes back to the house. If she doesn't show up soon, we'll call my uncle and get people looking for her. Hopefully, all we'll have to do is embarrass her when she shows up at the house." Cat opened her soup and drank it straight out of the thermos. She was starving and the sandwich had only made her hungrier.

"Sometimes I don't get people." He stood and nodded to the food. "I'm grabbing another sandwich before Shauna packs the rest up. Let me know if you need my help."

Cat wondered how to handle Jewel's absence. The woman was an adult. On the other hand, people got hurt and died out here. A point that Cat thought she'd made clear before they'd left the house. She'd call Uncle Pete when they got back to the house. At least then if

Jewel was still missing, he could get someone out to look for her before the storm hit. Maybe Seth would find her on the trail and she'd be back at the house writing when they arrived.

"Hope for the best, plan for the worst," Cat muttered as she finished her lunch.

As they were getting ready to return to the trailhead, Shauna stopped Cat. "If Seth doesn't find her on the trail and we don't find her on the road as we're heading home, I'll call Pete. He may not do anything for a while, but I think he should make the call, right?"

Cat nodded. "I was going to call when we got back, but I think your timeline makes more sense. Especially if she got hurt on the trail."

"Okay, we'll see you when you get back. I've got the chicken pot pies all ready to go into the oven for dinner. Our food costs are going to be higher this retreat since we're feeding them a lot more." Shauna zipped up the last soft-sided cooler and put it over her shoulder. "Be careful going back."

"Definitely." Cat hurried to catch up with Deek who was standing by the trail waving her over.

Cat and the group made good time going down the hill and when they arrived at the trailhead, Seth was just pulling in the parking lot. He opened all the doors and the back. "There's hot coffee thermos and cookies in the back if you need sustenance."

"Seth, you're an angel," Piper took off her snowshoes. "What do I do with these? I'm definitely not taking them home."

"Put your snowshoes in the back and keep on your snowsuit. We'll hang them up in the lobby this week in case you want to take another trip out. Or if we get a lot of snow, you can get to the library on your own." Seth pointed to the van and the group slowly made their way there, following Piper.

Cat pulled off her snowshoes and waited for them to leave. "Have you found her?"

Seth shook his head. "Shauna asked me to tell you that she's called Pete. He said not to worry, he'll deal with it."

"Does that mean he'll go looking?" Cat waited for an answer before she went to get a coffee of her own.

"Yes. He was organizing a team. He wants to chat with Hank though, so we're supposed to take him to the house. Your uncle will pick him up there and take him back to his car." Seth smiled. "I think someone's going to get a stern talking to."

Cat nodded and they walked back to the van. She grabbed her coffee and let Hank know about the plan. The fear on his face was almost worth losing a writer over.

When they got back to the house, a Jeep pulled into the driveway after them. As Cat got out, she saw it was Shirley and Linda. Cat motioned for the others to go inside and warm up as she went over to the passenger door to update Linda. Instead, she found a crying Linda in her arms.

"Oh, Cat, it was horrible," Linda sobbed into her shoulder.

Cat looked over at Shirley who had climbed out of the driver's seat and was now standing next to them.

"Let's get inside, Linda, okay? You might be going into shock." Shirley helped Cat get Linda to the door, but then Deek and Seth rushed out.

"We'll take her to her room." Seth met Cat's gaze. "Maybe send Shauna up to help get her settled?"

"I will." She followed them into the house with Shirley by her side. When she reached the kitchen, she relayed Seth's request and watched as Shauna hurried out of the kitchen to follow the men.

Shirley sank into a kitchen chair and started taking off her snow-suit. "I called Pete as soon as we got service. He should be here in a few minutes."

"Shirley, what happened? I thought you guys were going to her cabin."

"Well, it took me a while to find her since she'd gotten lost on the roads up to the cabin. We parked her car at the Forest Station road and then we drove up to the trailhead for Harris Hollow. When we got to the cabin, there was a light in the window." Shirley stood and went to pour herself a cup of coffee. "I thought I left this all behind when I retired."

"Shirley, what did you find?" Cat hoped no one had been squatting in the cabin. Desperate people did desperate things.

Shirley took a sip of coffee as she sat down. "Cat, there was a woman on the floor. She'd been hit with a fireplace poker. It was still next to her. She looked like she was sleeping but she must have hit her head going down or the blow from the poker was enough. Cat, she was dead."

Cat leaned back in her chair. "That's awful. And worse, now we have a murder and a missing woman. Uncle Pete's going to be busy this week."

Shirley shook her head. "You don't have a missing woman. Linda told me that she knew the woman. That it was that other writer, Jewel. The one that said she had an affair with Linda's husband."

CHAPTER
FOUR

Uncle Pete had asked all the writers to go to their rooms when he arrived. He then sent his deputy to start the interviews. Cat was sent to her office, and Shauna was in the kitchen, finishing dinner. Seth was in his apartment, resting. Hank was Uncle Pete's first interview and he was in the living room.

Uncle Pete came up to her office a few minutes later. She'd seen Hank get in the police car and leave. She should have been writing, but instead, she'd been pacing. At least this murder hadn't happened in the house. But it had still centered around Jewel and Linda. Cat should have sent Jewel home last night after the fight. At least she'd be alive.

Uncle Pete handed her a carafe and a cup. And then he'd set down a basket of cookies. "Shauna sent up some food. I've already chatted with her so she'll be bringing everyone their dinner to their rooms. She said you and Seth were the last on her list, so she hoped this would keep you."

"I can't believe Jewel is dead. I'm kicking myself for not sending her home after the fight last night." Cat poured herself a cup of what appeared to be the special mix of Warm Springs Hot Cocoa that Shauna made specifically for retreat weeks. "Do you want some?"

"I'm good. Shirley went home and she's cooking. So as soon as we get this put away for the night, I'll be heading there." He glanced at his watch. "After I visit the cabin. You keep me busy with your writer friends."

"Any idea who killed her?" Cat sipped the cocoa and closed her eyes. The sweet warmth was exactly what she needed.

"Besides your friend, Linda Cook?" He shrugged when Cat opened her eyes and glared at him. "The woman does seem to be at the wrong place at the wrong time. Tell me about the fight."

Cat went through the fight and what she knew from the time the two women came onto the property until now. "I still want to kill Hank for sending her off on her own. He should be punished for that."

"She didn't get lost or die from frostbite, Cat. Believe me, I'm going to make sure Mr. Rogers doesn't lead another group into the woods. He's a menace, but he didn't kill Ms. Doan." He took a cookie out of the basket as he stood. "Let me know if you hear about anything else that occurred between the women or about Jewel Doan specifically. I think I'm going to have to figure out if this affair was real. Have you heard anything about Tom Cook having other women around?"

Cat shook her head. "No, but he attended Covington before me and became famous when I lived in California. The only time I met him was right before he was murdered here."

"Okay, well, let me know. Shirley's leaving next Monday, can we do a family dinner on Sunday?" Uncle Pete switched subjects quickly.

"I'll let Shauna know." Cat stood and followed her uncle to the door.

"And Seth. He's almost family." Uncle Pete smiled. "Oh, and you can come downstairs and help Shauna with the dinners. You don't have to stay in your office now."

"Thanks, Dad. I promise I won't break curfew again," Cat joked as she followed him to the second floor where he'd do more interviews.

"I wish life was that simple around you." Uncle Pete leaned over and kissed Cat on the cheek. "Please stay safe. I don't like this situation."

Cat hurried downstairs to the kitchen and Shauna. "What can I help with?"

"Well, let's feed the new writers first. Pete said he'd start there so hopefully, we can time it so he's just left their rooms. He said he'd text when the first one was done." She pointed to the four trays on the table. "Then we'll do the returning guests and have a family meal in the kitchen when he finishes with Seth. Is Pete staying for dinner?"

Cat shook her head and explained that Shirley was cooking. And when Cat asked about Sunday dinner. Shauna went over and added it to her monthly calendar. "We'll do something special. Like a ham. And scalloped potatoes. We'll send Shirley off with a meal that makes her miss us."

"You and food," Cat took the salad and filled four bowls for the trays. Then she worked on rolls and butter. Shauna was cutting cheesecake and drizzling chocolate on top for the dessert. When her phone buzzed, she pulled a pot pie out of the warming oven. "Take this first tray to Wilder. Oh, and grab a Coke for his tray out of the fridge, please."

Cat grabbed the soda and then picked up the tray. "I'll have so many steps this week I won't have to get out of bed next week at all."

By the time Uncle Pete had talked to all the writers Cat had delivered all the dinners and was in the kitchen eating with Shauna and Seth. Deek had volunteered to run a writing sprint that night in the living room. Uncle Pete came into the kitchen before he left. Cat saw the weariness in his posture. "Hey, don't tell me you're still running out to the cabin tonight. It's after six."

"No rest for the wicked," He smiled as Shauna handed him a thermos of coffee. "Thank you, Miss Shauna. I'm sorry my niece's retreats tend to bring in problem children for you to deal with."

"Hey, this is not my fault. If you want to blame someone, look at Hank. He let Jewel take off without adult supervision." Cat knew her uncle was kidding, but she was starting to take the retreat's reputation as murder center of the Western United States a little personally. "According to Wilder, my retreat should be booked solid this year after this murder. I don't understand the draw. I'd be canceling my reservation if I heard about all these murders."

"You've said it before, writers are a different sort of crazy." Seth broke into his pot pie and the steam floated upward. "Pete, you're sure you're not hungry?"

"I didn't say that. I said Shirley's cooking. I don't want to tell her I ate with you guys and left her alone at the house while I did it." He glanced over at the brownies on a tray ready to go out to the dining room for writing treats. "But I wouldn't say no to a couple of those for the ride."

"You've got it," Shauna stood and put a few cookies and brownies into a Tupperware container. "This way, you can share if there are any left when you get home."

"Just don't mention how many you sent to Shirley." He held up his coffee. "I need to get going, but Cat, Shirley wants to know if she can come over and write with your retreat guests this week. She figures rightly that I'll be swamped at work now that this happened."

"That would be great. We kept the attendance of the retreat low so we could evaluate what worked and what didn't. She can give us another perspective." Cat saw Seth staring at her. "Oh, and it would be great to see her anyway. She's always welcome."

"That was a good save." Uncle Pete chuckled. "I'll drop her off in the morning on my way to the station. Thank you."

"Shirley's family," Shauna added as she sat. "You know she doesn't have to ask."

After Uncle Pete left, Cat muttered. "Shirley's not family, yet."

"She might as well be," Seth rubbed Cat's back. "And when she is, nothing's going to change between you and your uncle."

"Tell me that after she gets him to quit and move to the wilds of Alaska." Cat met Seth's gaze. "I know, I'm being selfish, but I'll miss seeing him around here."

MONDAY MORNING CAT woke up to find that the storm had left a couple of inches of snow and had cleared out of the area. As long as the snowplows got through to all the streets, the writers should have no problem getting to the library for Miss Applebome's welcome lecture. The three, now, four retreat guests would also have a library pass for the week. But instead of getting one in their name, their passes and library privileges were all tied to the retreat. So she had cards for retreat guests which had been put in their welcome packets. She'd give one to Shirley at breakfast and remind everyone about the library session. New retreat guests were mandatory to get their temporary library cards but reunion guests were optional.

Cat figured Miss Applebome would rather they didn't come for the session.

She slipped on a robe and slippers over her flannel pajamas and headed downstairs to grab a carafe of coffee and a cup from the kitchen. Words needed to be written, even if the world was in chaos. Maybe even because the world was in chaos. Writing calmed her down and made her happy. And while she worked, she didn't have to worry about poor Jewel.

Shauna was already in the kitchen and something sweet-smelling was baking in the oven.

"Good morning, I could smell the cinnamon when I came down the stairs." Cat walked over and got a carafe out of the cabinet and filled it with coffee. Then she grabbed a cup and filled it halfway. She sat down at the table. "What's on your schedule today?"

"Freshening rooms. After breakfast is done and cleaned up, I'll be baking more treats for the dining room. I love days like this where all I have to do is stay in the house and make it feel cozy." Shauna picked up her planner and brought it over to the table. "Are you and the guests walking over to the library? I need to let the reunion writers know that I'll be cleaning their rooms between ten and one, even if they don't go to the library."

"I'll ask who's not going to the library when I pop in at breakfast." Cat nodded to the planner. "Make a note to ask Uncle Pete if he's gotten ahold of Jewel's next of kin. Should we pack up her room?"

"I'm not sure he's cleared it, but I'll ask when he drops off Shirley. If someone's coming here, I'll keep her belongings here at the house. Otherwise, I'll get them shipped off. Probably after the retreat has ended." Shauna shook her head. "It's sad to think that she'll never finish her book or live her life."

"I'm sure Linda's glad she won't have to deal with a tell-all book about her husband." Cat finished her coffee. "Unless there's something else we need to deal with this morning, I need to get words down."

"Go be the reclusive author you always wanted to be." Shauna waved her off. "I've got the business side of this retreat handled. All you need to do now is sound smart."

"Which is harder than it looks," Cat stood and headed to the kitchen door. "Tell Uncle Pete I said hi and tell Shirley I'll see her at breakfast."

As she left the kitchen, she ran into Deek. He had a travel cup of coffee in one hand and a couple of cookies in the other. "Good morning. Are you claiming the den?"

"Yes, I am. I know there are more places in the west wing to write, but I love your den. It makes me feel like I'm Hemmingway or Fitzgerald or maybe even Sanderson." Deek grinned at her.

"Sanderson? Brandon Sanderson?" Cat thought she knew who

38

Deek was referring to. "I thought you were writing time travel not high fantasy."

"It's all in the same speculative fiction area. Besides, I like reading something a little different than what I'm writing. One, it makes me think about how I would have written a scene. And two, I don't accidentally think I had a brilliant breakthrough when really, someone else did the same thing."

"Good point. I don't read young adult paranormal academy books either. Especially when I'm in the drafting stage. Now this summer, I just swam in paranormal women's fiction. There are so many books in the new genre or subgenre." Cat leaned against the wall. She could talk books forever which is one reason she loved hosting the retreats. She got to talk to her people. People who loved reading and talking books as much as she did.

"Anyway, I better get in there. I'm hoping to finish this first draft this week while I'm here. I'm excited about the editing seminar tomorrow." Deek had plans other than talking his morning away. He waved and headed to the den.

Cat moved toward the stairs, like Deek, her literary heroes were genre writers. She'd tried reading the college prep reading list a few years ago and decided that if she was going to spend time reading, she wanted to read what she enjoyed or what taught her something. She'd even put a book down without finishing it or even pretending to have a plan to finish it later. Life was too short.

When she got to her office, she set a timer to remind her to visit the dining room during breakfast then poured herself a cup of coffee. She turned on her computer and loaded up the document. She consulted her notes from her last writing session and started telling the story through her fingertips. Life was good.

After breakfast, Cat waited in the hallway for the writers. Seth sat on the bench by the door, waiting with her.

"I can drive you all there you know." Seth had a book that he was reading while he waited. The boy typically could not stand still so his recovery from his quasi-military tour last year had gone in spurts and stops. He'd been sure he was being lazy, his doctor was concerned he was putting too much pressure on his recovery. And he wasn't the only one. So he'd started reading as something to do to pass the time.

"That's why you're on standby. I think the group is going to want to walk, but we'll see. They'll be walking a lot this week. If the weather turns really cold, we'll need to do drop off and pick-ups at the restaurants where they eat as well." Cat sat next to him. "Are you okay after yesterday?"

"Physically or mentally?" Seth put a gum wrapper in the book to hold his spot as he closed it.

"Both." She leaned against the wall. "I hate to claim bad luck, but we're on a bit of a streak. I bet if you put all the writer retreats out there, ours would win most murder adjacent."

"It's kind of a weird title but I guess it fits. Anyway, I'm hurting a little today. I think I'm just taking it easy unless someone needs transport. I'll be hanging out in my living room with Sam if you need me." He absently rubbed at his leg. "I hate feeling weak."

"You're getting stronger every month." Cat leaned her head on his shoulder. She wanted to tell him she'd told him so. That he shouldn't have gone away that last time. That he would have been fine if he'd just listened to her. But she held the would have, should have, could have's at bay. It wasn't fair to remind him.

"It's killing you not to say I told you so, isn't it?" Seth grinned at her.

"Just a little bit," Cat admitted.

"Hey guys, do you mind if I go to the library with the group," Shirley walked up to them. "I'd love to do some research this week. The book is almost finished, but then I think of something else and fall down the research rabbit hole."

Cat stood and handed her a library card. "Of course, you're welcome. I got you this to use as well. Just turn it back and any books you need us to return at the front desk. We'll get them back to the library."

Shirley took the card and put it in her back pocket. Then she gave Cat a bear hug. "That I didn't expect. You're pretty amazing. And your uncle loves you like you were his own."

"Thank you. I love Uncle Pete as well." Cat's mother's brother was the only family besides Seth and Shauna that she had in town since her mom and dad had moved to Florida a few years ago. She saw the other guests coming down the stairs. "And here's more of our caravan. Are you okay with walking to the library?"

"Of course," Shirley held out her watch. "I don't want to break my ten-thousand-step daily record. Especially not here."

Linda Cook was the last to arrive, but she wasn't dressed to walk to the library. "I'm not joining you today if that's okay."

"We're going to the Diner for lunch at noon if you want to join us there." Piper came over and gave Linda a hug. "You have to eat."

She smiled and nodded. "Maybe I will, but don't wait for me. I'll text Piper if I'm going to be able to make it. I promise, tomorrow I'll be back to my happy-go-lucky writer self."

Cat reminded her that Shauna needed to get into her room and Linda nodded. "I'll let her know when I'm out and about the house. I'm just not feeling very social today. And I still need to go to the cabin."

"Linda, let me do that. I'm sure Pete still has it off-limits. I'll figure out when I can get in there and if you still want to go, I'll go with you." A knock on the door made Cat turn. The florist was there with a vase filled with two dozen red roses.

"My contribution to the cause is here," Linda smiled and took the flowers from the delivery person.

Seth pulled out a ten and gave it to the driver. "Thanks."

"You really don't have to send flowers every month." Cat smiled as Linda brought them to her. "We love them of course, but..."

"Then just smile and say thank you." Linda took a rose out of the vase. "Go learn about the library. If you guys hang out here any longer, you're going to be late. And you know Miss Applebome."

"Walk or drive?" Seth pulled out a set of keys and rattled them over his head.

"As much as it pains me to say it, we've decided to walk to the library," Felix spoke for the group. He stretched his calf muscles. "I've been told that the best thing to do after a long walk in the woods is to keep moving."

"If you rest, you rust," Wilder added. "My Uncle Jim used to say that a lot."

"You've got a bunch of practical writers in this group," Seth teased Cat. "I'll go and let Sam out and get back to reading my book."

"Then let's go to the library," Cat waved everyone but Linda and Seth toward the front door. She saw that Ryan stood back, watching Linda. She paused by him. "As our Covington student, this library talk is optional. You don't have to go if you don't want to."

Andi paused by them. "You should come with us. Miss Applebome is different when she talks to us as writers rather than just students. It's like she believes in our ability to add to her collection one day."

Deek paused at the doorway as well. "I'm going to check out the time travel section. Miss Applebome said she curated a list for me to work off when I arrived."

"You've been talking with her from California?" Cat fell into step with the rest of the group and Ryan followed along. She guessed Andi's encouragement had made the difference. She thought Ryan was crushing on the local girl.

"We exchange emails now and then." He chuckled. "I like talking books with her. She's knowledgeable. It helps with my writing and my job."

Cat thought about the age and culture differences between the Colorado librarian and the California surfer dude. Maybe her writers' retreat brought all kinds of people together over their love of books.

If it wasn't shut down soon because of the abnormally high number of people who were killed in Aspen Hills during a session.

And now there was one more to add to that list. Jewel Doan. A woman Cat hadn't gotten to know at all, but she hadn't liked her from what she'd known. Uncle Pete could solve this mystery. She was going to focus on the retreat and her writing.

Period.

CHAPTER

FIVE

When the writers got back from lunch, Cat pulled Deek, Andi, Shirley, and Linda into the second-floor west-wing living room for a chat. Seth had set a fire in the stone fireplace. And Shauna had brought up coffee, hot chocolate, and treats. After they grabbed a beverage to warm up, Cat asked Shirley to introduce herself. "She'll be joining your group as a reunion participant, so please make sure to include her in your activities this week."

"Don't go out of your way, please." Shirley waved at the others. She explained that she was dating Cat's uncle and that with the investigation, she found herself with some time on her hands. She chuckled as she glanced at Cat. "That's actually how I wound up attending my first writing retreat as well. The good news is I'm almost done with a memoir about my time as a police officer in Alaska."

"So you kind of fit in with the whole non-fiction theme of this session's retreaters." Deek smiled. "Cat and I are the only true fiction writers this session."

"Dude, you're so dismissive. I write fiction." Andi playfully kicked him from her side of the couch where they were both sitting.

"You turn historical fact into fiction. So you all do a lot of research. Cat and I make everything up." Deek challenged.

"Sometimes, I take real facts and turn them into fiction. Like how I used the Covington campus as a model for the school Tori attends when she goes to college. I visited a boarding school before I wrote about her academy training." Cat shook her head. "I think I agree with Andi. There's nothing new in the world, it's just all how you spin it."

"Told you so," Andi stuck her tongue out at Deek.

Cat decided to change the subject. Andi Grammy had come to the retreat for the first time to look for her bio-father. A man Cat knew well, but Andi still didn't know at all. Dante Cornelio. The head of a crime mob family. And, who also happened to be the man Shauna was dating. Dante had been Cat's ex-husband's best friend and had never wanted to take over the family business. Until he found out that his brother was corrupt and had to be replaced.

It was a weird dichotomy that someone could be corrupt in a crime mob, but Cat guessed that even those organizations had rules to be followed. Andi looked like her dad. Dark and gorgeous, but she brought a lightness Cat had never seen in either of Andi's biological parents.

"Okay kids, let's stop fighting," Cat turned to the whiteboard she'd set up in the room. "I have a separate goal sheet for you guys. I wasn't sure what you'd be working on when you got here, so I thought we could talk about that this afternoon. Using a Covey technique, let's begin with what you want to have completed by Saturday when we go to dinner. Deek? Do you want to start?"

He pulled out a notebook. "I'm never short of ideas. I have the second book in my series done, but my agent is still shopping the first book in the series. I don't want to write a third, and then find out I can't sell the first book. I'd like to start a new project this week. Maybe leave here with a strong concept, an outline, and ten thousand words?"

Cat knew that Deek's goals would be high, but he was also deter-mined. She wrote down his name and new project/concept/out-line/10K on the whiteboard. "So you're going to have stages on your week. How long will it take to come up with the concept?"

"I can probably nail it down by the end of the day, with some help. I've got a lot of ideas," Deek admitted, holding up his notebook. "If I read off a tagline for each, can you guys tell me what you're most interested in?"

"We can, but I read women's fiction," Linda told him. "I might not be your best barometer."

"Let's get the house involved, then you pick the top ten. I can send it out to our writing group that meets at the bookstore and see if anyone there can chime in before midnight." Andi wrote down a note on her paper. "What do you think?"

"Aren't you afraid someone will steal one of the ideas?" Shirley asked. She looked stumped at the collaborative brainstorming going on.

"Shirley, if you and I wrote a book about a man who goes hunt-ing, the final product would be totally different," Cat explained. "Even if we start with all the same facts. Where he's living, if he's married, has kids, maybe he's a police officer. Given all that, I'd prob-ably pull from my dad's stories about hunting deer and how much he enjoyed his time walking through the forest, even if he didn't get a deer. Or time with his buddies. And it would probably wind up in a different fantasy dimension where the deer talked."

"Because you like writing paranormal," Linda added.

"Exactly." Cat pointed to Linda. "But Shirley, you would probably set your book in Alaska and the story would be about hunting a grizzly or man against nature. You'd probably focus on the stark reality of feeding a family rather than enjoying the scenery."

"And getting out of the backcountry before the weather turned dismal and they got stuck. Or maybe they would get stuck and have to fight their way out," Shirley mused on the idea.

"Or if you stayed in the non-fiction area, you'd write a book about hunters who had close calls while hunting in Alaska. Or how the native Indians hunted and how they preserved the meat for the long winter." Andi joined the conversation. "Besides, a true writer, someone who follows his muse, would never steal an idea."

Cat snorted. "I think it happens more than you believe. But I believe in karma. That people get what they put into this career. If you come in with a positive attitude and good intentions, the muse will reward you."

"Okay then, I'll get my list finalized before dinner and email it to you." Deek made a note and looked around the room. "Can we go through my list after this session ends?"

"Works for me," Shirley wrote something down on her paper. "Cat, I really enjoy crashing your retreats. I think I need to sponsor another writer or just throw money at you when I come."

"Let's just get your goals set today. We can talk about sponsorships another time." Cat wondered if she'd been missing out on a possible option. Having a non-profit that could sponsor someone who couldn't afford the trip to Colorado. Cat could just comp the room and board and entry fee, but even then, getting here was sometimes pricy. She wrote down enough of the idea in her notebook so she could go talk to Shauna and Seth later about the idea.

"I can see your wheels turning so I guess I hit on an idea for the retreat?" Shirley laughed and looked around the room. "You don't get this kind of energy sitting in your room writing alone."

"One of the reasons I started this retreat. You guys just think it's about me helping the guests." Cat teased as she finished writing her thoughts. She put down the pen and picked up the marker. "Honestly, it's all about feeding my muse. Let's hear your plan. Or do you still need time to think about one? We can move to Linda or Andi if you're not quite ready."

"That would be good," Shirley admitted as she looked over what she'd written down.

"I'll go then." Andi raised her hand. "Now that I'm out of school, I want to write something that would actually sell, so I've been reading a lot of mysteries. By the end of the week, I want Deek's goals, but a little less ambitious. I want a solid idea, including a subgenre of mystery I want to focus on. I want an outline and a list of characters, kind of. And I want a first chapter at least. I think better when I'm writing the story but I'd like to have bullet points to aim for as the plot progresses."

"That sounds doable. But let's say I'll have a solid idea, not I want..." Cat wrote down Andi's goals for the week. "Have you considered what plot structure you want to use?"

"Kind of, I brought all the how to structure books I bought over the last year." Andi walked over and grabbed a pile of books off the table. From what Cat could tell, she might have bought all of the plotting books available including a few Cat hadn't ever heard of.

"Maybe you could use one on writing the mystery and match it up to figuring out who killed Jewel." Deek ran a finger down the pile. "Here's the one that I've heard good things about. We could help you block out the clues. Like the fact that Jewel was killed in Linda's cabin. That's either a clue or a red herring."

Cat saw the flash of pain on Linda's face but it quickly went away. "Deek, I don't know..."

"Cat, hold on a second. Deek's right. I am a logical suspect in this murder. And if having Andi work through the clues and help your uncle find the true killer works, maybe we should think about doing it." Linda smiled over at Andi. "It would at least make this less frightening for me. I would know that at least you guys were on my side."

Shirley looked around the circle. "I want you to know that interfering with an investigation is a criminal act. So we would have to be careful and not mess up anything that Pete's working on. But I'm in. Especially if it gets the case off Pete's back sooner. I worry that he takes too much on during investigations."

Cat stared at her uncle's girlfriend. Of all the people in the room, Cat thought Shirley would be the voice of reason to pull the writers back away from getting involved. Or maybe Linda would talk them out of it. But everyone seemed to be on board with Deek's suggestion. "If you can't beat them, I guess I'll join in. But this doesn't excuse you from working on your own writing goals for the week."

Linda laughed and opened her notebook. "Yes, I will do my homework before I go play with my friends. Like I said before, I'm working on a memoir about my life with Tom. Of course, this Jewel situation is now part of it. I'm not sure how it will end up, but it's not something I can ignore. Especially not now. I've got most of the book written, I was finished up with the chapter on his death. But maybe I'll need a chapter about what happened next as well."

Cat wrote down Linda's name. "So I'm hearing that you want to finish the memoir this week and add a final chapter that you hadn't planned for. What are we looking at word count wise, five to ten thousand?"

Linda nodded, thoughtfully. "It may be more than two chapters, but I think around that. And a different summary. I thought I'd already written it, but with possible new information, I'll need to rethink it."

Cat wrote down a word count goal number for Linda and turned to Shirley. "Okay, your turn."

"The book is done but I'm not sure if it's enough. As I'm reading other memoirs, they feel more like fiction. My chapters feel more technical. I'd like to do an open mic night with everyone having a copy of the chapter I'm reading so they can take notes for suggestions." Shirley glanced at Cat. "Do you think that's possible?"

"We can do the first one tonight if you're ready. Ask Shauna to print out your first chapter and we'll make copies." Cat glanced at her watch. It was almost three. "Maybe you'll be up first thing after dinner?"

Deek grinned. "I love this idea. We've added a night once a month where people can read their works in progress to our writers' group at home. It's helping all of us."

"Then it's settled. I think having the reunion group here is going to add a lot to the writers' retreat. You guys are ready to take chances and level up." Cat picked up her phone and texted Shauna to expect

Shirley's first chapter. "Okay, Deek, the floor is yours. And if you want to start Andi's outline, we can do that afterward. I'll get more words tonight at the word sprint unless we're done before four and you guys want to do a round."

Deek opened his notebook. "I've got these all numbered. If you would want to read more, raise your hand. Any ideas that get more than three hands will go to the next round."

Cat settled in and let Deek take control of the group. She loved this part of the retreats which typically didn't start until later in the week. With the reunion group, they were already comfortable in being writers, now they could play with others.

SHIRLEY WAS BACK at the retreat fifteen minutes before seven. She came into the kitchen as they were finishing dinner and got the folder with the copies that Seth had made during a run to Covington's Office Space store. The college had a small store on campus that provided all kinds of services for students and the community including bookbinding, shipping, and copies. She pulled out the top set and shook her head. "I'm not sure about this."

"You'll do great," Cat assured her. "Seth and Shauna are joining the group tonight for your reading and Deek's idea vote. Then they're leaving when we do sprints."

"I might stay for a sprint round too," Shauna said as she cleaned off the table. "I need to write introductions for each of my chapters. My agent wants to shop this book, so we have to have it all pretty to send out."

"Well, I'm going to watch a game with Sam," Seth said as he took his plate to the sink. "I have nothing to write about."

"I'm sure that's not true, Seth." Shirley smiled at him. "But I have to ask, you don't have an extra room this week, do you? Pete's not too happy I'm getting into this retreat. I explained that it was his idea to keep me busy, but I guess he wanted someone at his beck and call.

We're going to dinner after my reading so I might need a place to stay."

"I'm sure you won't, but yes, we have a room on the third floor with us," Shauna squeezed Shirley's shoulder. "Tell Pete that we love him and to stop being an old grumpy bear."

Shirley laughed at the image. "You guys are the best."

After she left to go set up in the living room, and probably practice reading her chapter aloud, Cat finished clearing the table. "You don't think Uncle Pete's really mad at her, right?"

Seth shook his head. "He's probably just tired from the investigation. It's easier to just take your frustration out on the one you love. You know they aren't going to judge you for being a jerk."

"Unless it happens too much," Shauna warned. "Anyway, help me carry out these treat trays and set up the dining room. Seth and I will be in our seats exactly at seven, but Cat, you probably need to go play with your writers."

"Being creative isn't playing, it's hard work. Especially when you're starting out. Then if you keep at it, sometimes it feels like playing." Cat picked up a tray. "I'm proud of Shirley standing up for the time she needs. Even if Uncle Pete isn't."

"Oh, I think he's proud of her, he's just feeling guilty that his job is taking him away from spending time with her." Seth followed her out into the hallway, carrying two trays. Shauna followed them.

Cat set hers down on the sideboard. "Well, let's hope. I like Shirley."

"Unless she takes Pete off to the wilds of Alaska, right?" Shauna reminded her.

"Yeah, there's that." Cat grabbed a peanut butter cookie and headed to the living room. Most everyone was already there and chatting among themselves. She glanced at the whiteboard. The retreat guests still needed to post their goals. They had a lot to fit in tonight.

"Cat, the library is beautiful. And all those books," Piper took a deep breath. "It was like stepping into my own private library."

"I'm glad you enjoyed it. I hope you make use of it while you're here." Cat took her place at the lectern. "Welcome, we have a lot to do this evening. First up, we're having a reunion guest who is needing some critique of her memoir. Remember to be kind, but clear in your comments. Shirley will let you know what she's looking for, but I'm sure she'd appreciate additional comments if you have them. Then Deek, another reunion guest, needs a vote on some book ideas. He'll let you know exactly what he needs after Shirley's done. Then we'll do a goal setting discussion for the week for retreat guests. And after we have word count goals set, we'll do at least one-word sprint. This is not college. You are not graded on attendance. That being said, the more you participate, the more you'll get out of the week."

Seth and Shauna walked in with a box of clipboards and pens. They took one each and passed it down the line. Shauna laughed, "So what Cat's telling you is you are graded on attendance."

"Okay, we're all here. Shirley, you're up." Cat sat down and smiled at Shirley who had just turned stark white. *Oh, please don't throw up or pass out.*

Cat and the group waited for Shirley to start. She handed the folder to Andi who was sitting closest to the lectern. "Okay, I'm Shirley. My book is supposed to be a funny memoir of my time as an Alaskan police detective, but I feel like I'm missing the story threads. Any help with what to focus on, would be appreciated."

"Do you want us to point out grammar or typo errors?" Andi asked, her pen in the air.

Shirley nodded. "Please. I didn't major in English in college. I got a criminal justice degree. Anyway, if we're ready?"

Nods came around the room.

"Okay, here goes nothing. Chapter One." Shirley started reading and the room got quiet.

Cat listened to Shirley read and then noticed a movement from her left. Linda's foot bouncing up and down. Nerves or something more? Like guilt.

CHAPTER

SIX

The next morning, Cat went down for her coffee and to grab something sweet. She should wait for breakfast, but writing and snacking went together. At least on retreat weeks. Other days, she would grab coffee then write until the muse left the building or Shauna came up to let her know that lunch was ready. Some days, the muse never showed up at all. On those days after writing a couple hundred words, she'd give up and work on marketing or scheduling. But every morning started here, in Shauna's kitchen.

Today was no different. Shauna was busy baking for the guests. She put a lot into the one meal that the retreat provided and tried to come up with different themes, to keep the food interesting. Today, she was doing a play on building your own pigs in a blanket. The smells from the sausage and maple syrup made Cat's stomach growl as soon as she came into the kitchen.

"So Shirley's book is good, don't you think?" Shauna asked as she put pancakes and sausages on a plate, then covered it with butter and hot syrup. She held out the plate. "Ready for breakfast?"

"Just because you asked so nicely, yes." Cat grabbed the plate and sat down at the table. She took a bite and groaned. "This is so good. And yes, I think Shirley has all the parts, she just needs to make it more conversational."

"Well, they gave her a lot of suggestions on ways to do that." Shauna sat down with her plate. "I'm glad you like breakfast. I thought it would be fun. Have you noticed that the retreat feels different this time? More involved."

"I did notice that. It's the reunion guests. They are ready for the work at the beginning. When it's just the newbies, they don't understand what they can do or how the group can work together. I've never even thought about doing an open mic session. We should add it in to the schedule, maybe on Fridays for groups that don't have reunion guests. That would give them time to warm up to each other." Cat dug into the pancakes. They were so good. "And of course, they want to help investigate Jewel's murder. Uncle Pete is going to be mad that I didn't stop them."

"And probably mad at Shirley too. Maybe I should refresh Seth's old room. Shirley doesn't seem like the type to step away from something like this." Shauna stood and went to the desk, writing a note on her calendar.

"I'm betting she can get Uncle Pete to see her side. She said she wanted to keep us out of trouble." Cat stood and poured herself a glass of orange juice.

"Us? So you're helping?" Shauna got them coffee and brought it to the table.

"Maybe. I guess." Cat squirmed in her chair. "Okay, yes. I have the sleuthing bug. Besides, I feel guilty for not kicking Jewel out that first night. We need a one-strike policy on fighting."

"Woulda, coulda, shoulda. Don't do that to yourself." Shauna sipped her coffee. "So we have two sessions today, not counting the night games?"

"Night games, that's a good name for it." Cat set down her fork. "Okay, so we have a business school professor, Mike Presley, coming by to talk about goal setting and small business mission statements.

I've asked him to focus his discussion on one-person endeavors like authors, but it's in the air what the writers might ask. Three of the new retreaters are writing books about different aspects of goal setting. Everyone wants to be the new *Atomic Habits*."

Shauna had stood and grabbed her planner. "He's at ten, right? I'm coming to that session. I didn't love that book like you did, so maybe having someone talk about planning and goal setting will give me some ideas. What about the reunion guests? Is their session the same time?"

"Actually, no. I have Kathy Meyers coming at three to talk about editing. I thought more of the reunion writers would be at that stage, but Deek and Andi are starting new projects this week. And both groups can attend either session." Cat finished her breakfast. "And if I'm going to get any writing done today, I need to get in my office before someone comes through that door and needs something."

As she rinsed her plate, Seth came in the kitchen door. "Good morning, all."

"Good morning, Seth." Cat walked over and kissed him. Doctor Hollis had told her she wasn't affectionate enough. In her defense, she thought she was just busy. Especially the week of a retreat and while she was writing. "I'm heading upstairs to write. Do you need something from me before I go?"

He laughed and went over to pour himself coffee. "You're following Dr. Hollis's rule book for a positive first encounter each and every day, aren't you."

"I'm trying," Cat wanted to go write, but she slowed her breathing. She could act like she had all the time in the world for Seth. Even if it wasn't true.

"Anyway, Linda asked me if I could take her to her cabin sometime before the week's over. I told her it was up to Pete on when he released the scene." He sipped his coffee. "Maybe you might want to come with us."

Cat felt her heart racing. Going to the scene would give her information about how Jewel was killed. And she could take pictures of the area. Maybe even find a clue. She paused, Shauna was right, she was hooked on this investigation thing. "I'd like to go with you. Let me know when you're going. My calendar's here on the counter. Besides retreat things, I'm free anytime."

"Well, I don't think it's going to be today. Linda wanted to go to the sessions, but maybe Wednesday if Pete clears it. I'll keep you in the loop." He nodded to the stove. "Okay if I eat now? I need to go over and clean Mrs. Rice's driveway. She's coming home from the cruise at the end of the week. I'd like to get it cleared before we get more snow to move."

"And on that happy note, I'm going upstairs to write." Cat took the carafe and cup that Shauna had sitting by the door. Mrs. Rice was their next-door neighbor and although she loved Shauna and Seth, Cat wasn't one of her favorite people. She wasn't even sure that she'd known the woman was out of town. She saw Ryan in the hallway, laptop in hand, heading to the west wing. "Good morning, Ryan. Where are you heading so early?"

He blushed and the red went up to his blond hair. "Andi said I could come up to the west living room and write with her. If that's okay."

Cat shrugged. She had expected the groups to naturally divide, but it looked more like they were bonding together. "Sure, it's not a problem. Tell Andi I said good morning."

As she headed up the stairwell, she glanced at her watch. Not even seven and at least three of the people in the old Victorian were getting ready to write. This was exactly what she'd imagined when she started the writers' retreat. People of the same mind. People who loved books, words, reading, and writing. Cat was in writer's heaven.

As long as you didn't think about the murder.

∿

PROFESSOR MIKE PRESLEY WAS A DREAMBOAT. Even Shauna had taken a pause when she'd stepped into the living room and saw the female retreat guests crowding around him at the lectern. She met Cat at the back of the room and sat down. "Did you know he looked a lot like Elvis?"

"I've never met him before." Cat smiled as the others came into the room. The men, glanced at the crowd, frowned, then found a seat. Shirley was already sitting next to Cat.

"He's pretty, but sometimes, that's not a good thing." Shirley said to Shauna as she continued to stare. "Give me someone with character, like Pete, any day of the week."

"Pete's handsome, but this guy should be in the movies." Shauna laughed at the glare Shirley gave her. "What? It's true. I bet he has a ton of groupies that take his class and fail because they can't pay attention."

Linda was the last to come into the room and she shut the door behind her after counting the filled seats. She took a look at Professor Presley, raised her eyebrows then came straight back to sit next to Shirley on Cat's right. "Covington does tend to hire the most interesting professors available."

Cat turned toward Linda. "You realize I taught at Covington."

"I rest my case," Linda responded and opened her notebook.

Cat caught the professor's gaze and he sent Andi and Piper to their seats in the front row. Then he introduced himself. "I'm here to talk to you about goal setting and mission statements. Most people see goals as resolutions. They pick some target that they think they want to reach, put their head down, and go for it. When they fail, it's because they climbed a tree in a forest, but they picked the wrong tree to get them to their goal."

"Good analogy," Shauna whispered to Cat.

She ignored her friend.

"After today, you'll be able to use my five-step process to choose a goal. Then all you have to do is follow the path you set down to reach it. Are we ready to begin?" Professor Presley didn't wait for an answer, he turned to the flip charts he'd brought along. And introduced his book.

The one thing the business department hadn't mentioned about Professor Presley was he taught his classes using textbooks he'd written himself. There were no mentions of other, related books that Cat could have listed off in a heartbeat. She was a bit of a goal setting super nerd and had a ton of books she'd read on the shelves in the den. She'd send the group there after the professor left the building to give at least a different viewpoint on the practice. She didn't like people who said this is the way and the only way. *Follow me.* It made her twitch.

So by the end of the session when the professor had pulled out a stack of books and told them he'd sell anyone a signed copy who wanted more information, Cat was furious. She stood and took over the lectern. "Thank you so much for your presentation, Professor Presley. If you want more reading material, check out the books I have on the shelves where Deek's writing. I'm sure he won't mind you popping in. And of course, there's the library and on Friday, we'll be at the bookstore. Have a great lunch you guys. The next presenter will be here at three talking about editing."

She turned to Professor Presley. "I didn't realize you were bringing books to sell."

He laughed like it wasn't a big deal. "I always bring books. If I sell one, it's a win for me. One more follower of my system. Is there a problem?"

Cat considered her next words. She hadn't said he couldn't sell his books. "I guess I was looking for more of an overview of goal setting."

"Well, these are smart people. They need a quick and dirty process so they can go on with their real passion, writing." He turned and Andi and Piper were standing by the desk where he had set out his books. "Oh, I've got questions."

Cat left the room and met up with Shauna. "Do you mind watching the professor and helping him out. I can't believe the college sent him. And I still have to pay him for his time."

"He wasn't that bad, Cat." Shauna reached out to touch her arm trying to calm her. "I liked having a clear-cut process. I don't need all the options, just one I can use."

Cat realized she was reacting to what she'd expected, not what others needed. "You're right. I'm not sure why I'm so jumpy today."

"Mid-retreat with a murder thrown in. It messes with your head." Shauna nodded to the room. "Go workout or take a bath or something else to relax. I've got this. Lunch is at one."

Cat headed up to her office. She would be better off going through her emails or doing accounting or even filing rather than try to take a nap. If none of these calmed her down, she'd go to the basement and get on the treadmill. But she liked to leave it open during retreat weeks so her guests could use the gym if they wanted to without her hogging the machines.

In the middle of an email exchange about an upcoming book tour, she realized it was already almost one. She wrote down the definite dates for the stops she'd finalized and went downstairs with her planner. She'd update the house calendar. Maybe Seth might want to go with her on one or more of her trips. Normally he'd say he was too busy with handyman work around town, but with his limitations, he might just want to drive her to an event or help her with the session. A girl could hope.

When she got downstairs, Uncle Pete and Shirley were in the kitchen eating already. "Hey guys, why didn't you call me down? I didn't know you were coming for lunch."

Uncle Pete threw a side eyed look at Shirley. "I didn't come for lunch. I need to go through Jewel's room and possessions. I'll pack them up and take them to the station. No one's been in there, right?"

"I didn't even clean the room yesterday," Shauna replied as she sat a bowl of chili in front of Cat. "There's cornbread and butter to go with it."

"Thanks," Cat absently grabbed a square of still warm cornbread and slathered butter on it. "Did you find her next of kin?"

"Her brother is coming in from New Jersey to claim the body. Her folks are older and can't make the trip." Uncle Pete took a square of cornbread as well. "According to the family, Jewel worked in an administrative role in a car leasing business. No one knew anything about her writing a book."

"Did she tell her family about a relationship with Tom Cook?" Cat wondered.

He shook his head. "Again, according to family, at the beginning of last year, she had divorced her husband of ten years due to his cheating. They didn't think she was seeing anyone."

"Maybe she was keeping her relationships secret from her family. Sometimes people judge you when they hear divorce." Shauna sat down with them to eat.

"Maybe." Cat focused on eating. She'd been grumpy earlier with Professor Presley and she didn't want to make a repeat performance of her less than positive side. "Or maybe the guy just looked like Tom Cook."

Everyone at the table stared at her. Cat felt their attention and looked up. "What? It happens. You're always reading about people who are pretending to be someone famous because they look like a celebrity."

Shirley added, "There are cases with identical twin killers. Or one's a killer and one's a nice guy."

"Okay, barring a Tom Cook doppelganger, it looks like Jewel either lied about being in a relationship with a famous author or she was duped. I guess I should ask Linda if Tom had siblings." Uncle Pete pulled out his notebook and wrote the question down. "Now, can we talk about something besides the murder investigation that has me running twenty-four-seven?"

"Sure," Shauna grinned before she asked, "How about this snow? We're supposed to get another foot on Thursday."

"I'll probably need to drive the group to the library on Thursday and the bookstore on Friday." Seth walked into the kitchen. "I see you started without me."

"Seth, sit down. I'll get you some chili. I figured you'd need something warm after being out shoveling snow this morning." Shauna stood and went to the stove.

"You're the best, Shauna. Besides, Cat that is," Seth kissed Cat on her head, then sat down next to her, grabbing cornbread and taking a bite, without the butter. "Hey guys, what are we talking about besides the weather?"

Shauna set a bowl of chili in front of him. "We were talking about Pete's investigation, but he got a little squirmy when we got too involved so we're looking for a new conversation topic, better than just the weather."

Seth looked at Cat. "How was your new professor? Was it an interesting talk?"

"We're avoiding that topic too," Shauna broke in. "Cat wasn't pleased with the non-inclusive subject of his chat."

Seth shook his head. "Okay, then, what about you, Shirley? How's your visit so far and why the surprise drop-in? Was Alaska too cold and you wanted to feel the tropical snowstorms of Colorado?"

Shirley and Uncle Pete exchanged a glance. Then she took a breath. "My trip has been lovely and thank you all for letting me crash your retreat on a moment's notice. As for the reason I came, that should be obvious. I missed Pete."

He reached over and took her hand. "And I'm not helping by being busy with this investigation. I swear, as soon as I retire, you and I will be together so much that you'll get tired of hearing me talk."

"Pete, you're never going to retire and you know it." Shirley stood and took her bowl to the sink. "I'm going to go write for a while. I got a lot of great suggestions at last night's reading that I need to implement before I forget them or don't understand what the edit was saying. Pete, I'll see you tonight at the Diner for dinner at five?"

"I'll be there," Uncle Pete focused on his chili as Shirley left the kitchen.

No one said anything for a full minute. Finally, Cat broke the ice. "So you two are fighting? Over what, the investigation?"

"Not over the investigation. Shirley wants me to retire now. I want to wait for five more years to hit my top pension amount. The town and college have this agreement and the families, through the college, pitch in once you hit twenty years. It's a significant differ-ence. Like between traveling to Ohio for a week and going to Europe." He narrowed his eyes at Cat. "If you'd stop inviting trouble to your retreat, it might have been a quiet week for her to come and visit."

CHAPTER

SEVEN

The afternoon's editing seminar went smoothly and after it was over, most of the writers got together and left to eat at the Garnet. Shirley was meeting Uncle Pete. Linda was meeting a friend who taught English at the college, Sarah Warren. Cat had met Sarah when she taught at Covington, but they'd never developed any kind of relationship besides co-worker.

Shauna had taken Seth's meal to him in his apartment as he was dealing with spending the morning out in the cold shoveling snow. The man didn't know his limitations and so tonight, they were flaring up and teaching him a lesson.

Cat sat in the kitchen with Shauna going over the retreat so far. Shauna had made meatloaf and scalloped potatoes for dinner, one of Seth's favorites. If Cat didn't know the two were more like siblings, she would have been worried, but Shauna loved her and Seth like they'd all been born in the same family.

"If Jewel hadn't been killed, we could have called this trial run of the reunion and retreat mix a success. Right now, I think things are going well, but anytime there's a murder, it messes with the writing flow. I can tell you right now that the per-person word count for this retreat will be lower than a retreat where there's not a murder. No matter what Wilder says about people wanting to attend a murder retreat. It messes with the writing mojo." Cat glanced at her notebook where they were planning for February's All About Love retreat. Shauna had only accepted romance writers into that themed retreat. "Maybe we should throw the idea out on the website with a caveat that if they are randomly in a murder retreat, there's an additional hundred dollar up charge."

"Unless you're the victim," Shauna added.

"That is so wrong," Cat started laughing, and releasing some of that tension felt good. "Do you want to run the Night Games as you called it tonight? I'm going to go upstairs and soak in a bath until all the negativity washes away. I can ask Deek if you're busy."

"No, I can run it. I told you I would help with these." Shauna made a note on her calendar. "And I want to make some kind of writing part of my regular activities, so this will help."

As Cat waited for the tub to fill, she pulled up Google and looked up Tom Cook's Wiki page. Married, Linda. Two kids. And his mom was still alive as was a sister and a brother. She then searched for Boyd Cook. She found two references, both listing him as Tom's brother. No work history, no awards. No fame. Google had him living in Connecticut. When she tightened the search to Boyd Cook, Connecticut, there was a reference to his coaching a debate team at Stamford High School.

She tried to find a picture of him, but the only one she found with the debate team wasn't clear. Could Boyd have been the 'Cook' boy that Jewel had a relationship with? And if so, where would they have met? New Jersey wasn't exactly close to Connecticut but it wasn't like she was in Alaska or on the moon. And even if he was the one Jewel had been seeing, it didn't mean he'd killed her.

She sank into her bath and tried to think of something else. Something to make her relax. Like butterflies or soft music. Or candles, she should have lit candles before getting in the tub. Or at least started some music. Shoulda, Coulda, Woulda. Shauna would scold her for worrying about something she couldn't change. At least not now. Cat sank lower into the water and decided to take Shauna's imaginary advice and worry about it tomorrow.

~

WEDNESDAY MORNING, Cat felt more like herself. She wondered if she'd been coming down with something. Or if it was a delayed reaction to Sunday's snowshoeing outing. Either way, the sun was shining brightly this morning and it matched her mood. She hurried downstairs for coffee so she could get back to her office and start writing.

Shauna was in the kitchen, humming along to a song on the radio. She was baking this morning. A breakfast casserole from the smell. And, she must have already made muffins because Cat could smell the apple cinnamon. But she wasn't here for the food, she needed coffee.

Shauna must have heard her coming because she turned and handed Cat a cup filled with coffee. "Good morning. Are you better today?"

"I'm a positive light in a world of opportunity." Cat laughed as she took the cup. "How did the Night Games go?"

"You're dead set on calling it that, aren't you?" Shauna brought her cup over to the table and sat down.

Cat laughed. "It's a fun name. I'm surprised we didn't come up with something before. And it sounds like a session I'd want to go to if I was retreating."

"Well, the night games were a success. Linda wants to read tonight, so I told her I'd get her copies made. I let the group know that we only have three more opportunities for group feedback – Thursday to Saturday. So far no one jumped at the idea, but I could see the wheels turning." Shauna sipped her coffee. "I think adding this option to the reunion guests gives the retreaters confidence that they *can* write and that they know enough to help others."

"Building on each other's success, I like it." Cat leaned back. "I played with an idea last night."

"For a new book?" Shauna's eyes lit up. "Tell me more."

Cat laughed and shook her head. "Sorry to disappoint you. I was thinking about Jewel and a fake Tom. His brother, Boyd, must teach at a Connecticut high school. He's a debate coach. The town isn't that far from New York. What if they met there, in the city, since Jewel is from New Jersey? And he pretends to be his famous brother."

"And they have an affair." Shauna nodded. "It could work."

"Which would explain one mystery, but not who killed Jewel. Unless she told him she was coming here and confronting Linda." Cat frowned as she warmed her hands around the coffee cup. "But we don't release who's coming to the retreat, do we?"

Shauna answered the question. "We do. I send a get to know you chat invite a month before the retreat, just in case they want to meet up during the travel stage or share a cab or something. Maybe I shouldn't?"

"Don't throw the baby out with the bath water." Cat grinned as Shauna rolled her eyes. "We don't have any proof that Boyd is the guy that Jewel was seeing. Her folks don't even think she was seeing anyone. Right now, all we have are a lot of maybes."

"Well, it's a possible answer for why Linda had no clue Tom was cheating. He wasn't." Shauna got up when a buzzer went off and took two casseroles out of the oven. "Do you want to eat now or later?"

"Later. I need to write. Then I'll eat before my seminar at ten. And after that, I'll ask Linda about Boyd. Maybe she'll be able to link Boyd and Jewel. Then Uncle Pete can call Boyd and see if he is a liar, a cheat, and a killer. One can only hope." Cat stood and grabbed the carafe. "Thanks for handling the group last night. Did you get a lot of words in?"

"Surprisingly, I got three recipe introductions done. I'll need to edit them and make sure the stories flow, but it was fun." Shauna pulled out a large bowl. "Take one of those muffins with you. I can't promise I'll still have any when you come back down."

"Sold." Cat grabbed a muffin and balanced it in her now empty cup. She headed upstairs to focus on her work in progress and leave everything else behind. She had a ritual as she walked the stairs to go work. Coffee in hand, she used the different floors as reminders to leave everything else, and everyone else behind. This was her time. And she wanted to spend it writing. She'd deal with the rest of the world later.

A few hours later, after she closed the Word document where she was writing her current book, she sent the file to herself. She was planning on attending the Night Games tonight and getting more words done. Shauna could run the event, Cat didn't have to be the face of every activity they did. For now, she needed to pull the file with her seminar notes. She kept every question and most of the answers in the file just in case someone asked the same question. At a normal retreat, she'd use at least ten of the already answered questions so she wanted to make sure the answers were still true. Something she thought she knew as fact last year might not be the same today. Especially when they were talking about the publishing business.

If she changed something, she'd change it in her Word file for the talk and print out a new copy when she was done with her review. Most months, this review only took a few minutes, but she always allowed at least thirty minutes to the process. Today, she kept returning to what she was doing this year. What changes did she need to make to her schedule, to her career? She liked what she was writing, but a successful author she'd heard lecture many years ago had one nugget of gold in his talk. He said to always have something in your pocket or a project out being shopped at all times.

She didn't have a spec project in her pocket, and she needed one. It would make her relax about what might happen in the future with sales. And when she was relaxed, she wrote better. As she realized this, she pulled up her calendar and blocked off a week next month.

She'd spend it in Denver or somewhere else, just thinking about what she wanted to happen in her career and planning out this spec project. Then she'd schedule time to write it.

As she looked for a week on the calendar, she saw that Shauna had already blocked off a week for their group vacation between now and February's retreat. Seth had blocked off Valentine's Day on her calendar. And of course, the next retreat was already there. She had the week before a deadline blocked as well as a full week for the next release.

Carving out time for a special project was going to take some creative time management. But she knew she'd feel better, more in control of her career as soon as it was done. And that was the key to being able to keep up this career. Not resting on your last book or what was coming. You needed to fight for a place for your stories in the world and in your own life.

By the time she found her planning week and had set up a short-term rental, her stomach was growling. She'd booked a house in Arizona, hoping the change of scenery would spark her creativity. She sent a note and link to Shauna and Seth, letting them know she'd be gone that week. She thought about inviting them, but wanted to focus on her and her career, not other people.

When she got down to the kitchen to eat, it was empty. Shauna had left a note saying she'd gone into town for supplies and Seth had followed her note on the whiteboard with one of his own saying he was heading to pick up Mrs. Rice's cat from the boarder. He wasn't doing well there so Seth was bringing him back to the house to stay with him.

"Sam will freak out," Cat said to the empty kitchen as she pulled out the breakfast casserole from the fridge and cut herself a large piece to microwave. A small meow came from the open basement door. Seth had moved Angelica and her four now adult kittens from the barn to the basement when the weather dropped. Snow, Shauna's horse, had heater lamps to ward off the chill, but Seth had worried about the cats out in the cold so he'd brought them inside.

Angelica stepped into the kitchen, looking around to see if anyone else was there.

The cats seemed to know when retreat week arrived because they typically hid in the basement and avoided the new arrivals. Angelica was the more social of the group, but she even seemed to show up more after the retreat week was over.

"Hey girl," Cat leaned down and rubbed her back. "We're getting a visitor for a few days until Mrs. Rice comes home. You've probably already met him."

Cat couldn't remember what the cat's name was. Maybe she was the bad neighbor in the situation and not the nosy elderly woman next door. She focused on the cat with his owner and smiled. His name was Mr. Peeps. Happy with her discovery, Cat got her breakfast ready, adding a glass of orange juice to go with it. Then she pulled out a book and started reading.

Deek found her there a few minutes later. Angelica had been lying at her feet, but the cat hurried over to greet the newcomer. "Hi sweet girl. I haven't seen you in the den for a while."

"Angelica likes you. She typically runs from our writer friends." Cat closed her book and took her empty plate to the sink. "Do you need something?"

"The coffee's empty in the dining room. I thought I'd fill up before your session." He glanced around the kitchen. "I can make some if Shauna's not here."

"I can make a pot of coffee." Cat laughed as she filled the machine with water. "I know you all think Shauna is the magic food fairy, but when she's not here, I can even feed myself."

"I don't know. If I had a house where someone who wrote cookbooks lived with me, I think I'd just enjoy the ride." Deek glanced out the window at the snow. "I love visiting Colorado, especially this time of year, but I don't know if I could live here. I like wearing shorts all year long. I had to buy two new pair of pants for the retreat."

"Oh, the horrors of living in paradise." She reached for a carafe that was on the top shelf, but she was too short.

"Let me," Deek stepped closer and pulled down a silver carafe. "Just one?"

"Grab two. I don't want to put anyone asleep during my presentation." Cat took two cookie trays out of the fridge that Shauna had set up before she'd left for the store, just in case. "How's your book going? Did you settle on a plot?"

"Definitely. I've been writing since it hit me Monday night. I think it's a winner, but then, I always do. I'm such an optimist, it's kind of sad at times." Deek leaned on the counter as the coffee brewed. "I love my life. Working at the bookstore is the best. I've got writing the books to keep me busy. I thought leaving school would be hard. But I've found my niche."

"Now, all that needs to happen is your book goes viral and you become a famous author. Just don't forget to mention how vital attending the Warm Springs Writers' Retreat was to your development." Cat watched Angelica curl up at Deek's feet. The cat was in love.

"From your mouth to God's ears. Or whatever deity you call on." Deek reached down to rub Angelica's ears. "Of course, after seeing what happened to Tom Cook, I'm not sure I want to be famous. Linda's still struggling with his death. And Jewel, well, she was in love with the guy. Or she at least thought she was. I could see it in her aura."

Cat thought about Deek's observations. "I'm not a big believer in auras, but you think Jewel was grieving losing Tom?"

"She had sadness clouding her aura. The funny thing is the sadness usually shows as a grey cloud, and Linda's did. Jewel's cloud was more pink tone." He stood as the coffee pot finished. "I sent my mom an email asking about it. She's on a cruise, so I probably won't get an answer back before Sunday, but I'll let you know what I hear."

He filled the two carafes with coffee and headed to the door. "I'll come back for the cookies if it looks like we need more."

"Great. Thank you." Cat was lost in thought but she stopped him before he left the kitchen. "Hey, if you hear anything else about Jewel or her death, can you let me know? I'd like to know what's going on and I don't hear much stuck in my writer cave."

"That's the point, right?" He stood in the doorway, watching her. "But I'll keep you in the 411. Andi has been trying to put clues together, but she got distracted with her writing. The muse wants what the muse wants, right?"

Shirley came in right as Deek left. She held the door open as he took the coffee carafes. "And great minds think alike. Do we have more cookies I can take out? The offerings look a little bare."

"I've got two trays ready," Cat nodded to the counter. "How are things with you and Uncle Pete?"

"Oh, don't ask. He's grumpy but I'm blaming the mood on the murder. The college had denied any connection to the deceased so he's looking into who checked into the local bed and breakfast and hotels in the last week. He really doesn't want to falsely accuse Linda Cook, but honestly, as much as I like the woman, she'd be the first one on my suspect list."

"I can see why, but she wasn't at the cabin until after Jewel was killed." Cat thought that one point alone should help Linda get off her uncle's list.

"I couldn't find her for an hour that day. I know I went by the forest office at least once but she swears she was sitting there in the parking lot, trying to find an old email on her phone from Tom telling her about the time he had problems finding the cabin in the snow. She hoped the email had better landmarks." Shirley glanced at the door. "She could have killed Jewel and then gone to the parking lot to have an alibi. After that fight on Saturday night, she was mad enough to kill someone. And her cheating husband wasn't around."

CHAPTER
EIGHT

As Cat looked around the mixed group of new and returning authors, she felt emotion start to overwhelm her. She'd started the retreat a few years ago and it had already grown into something larger. Of course, that one internet site called the retreat, Colorado Murder Central, but no other news agencies had picked up the moniker. Probably due to the college's connections. She had to take a breath as she looked at the results of the idea she'd thrown up as a possible income source the first night she'd been sitting in the living room with Shauna, talking about what to do with the oversized Victorian. Cat had lost the house in the divorce and gotten it back in her late ex-husband's will.

Life was funny like that. Things happened that blessed your life and some that tore it apart. If she'd never left Michael and Aspen Hills in the first place, she wouldn't be here with Seth, again. The retreat wouldn't have existed. And she would have probably still been teaching at the college, uncertain of her writing ability and what books she wanted to write.

It was time to share her author knowledge with the group. And the important thing was to be completely honest with them.

"Welcome everyone to our *Chat with the Author* session. I'm here, not as an all-encompassing expert, but instead, someone who has been where you are and is still working in the industry and writing stories about her imaginary friends." She smiled at the writers gathered around her.

"And you're getting paid for your books. That's the important part. Tell us how to get seven-figure contracts so we can stop working for the man." Wilder Russ was in the front row with a notebook open and a pen in his hand.

"What worked five years ago, when I started, doesn't work now. Or at least I don't think it does all the time." Cat left the podium and sat in the chair next to it, looking out on the writers who were in the session. "You need to do the work, take the chances, and wish for a little pixie dust. And never give up. Because that's the only time when you have failed. So this is your time, besides giving you the keys to your million dollar best seller, what else do you want to talk about?"

Shauna had come home and was now standing at the flipchart, waiting to write down ideas. Cat used to do this and try to talk but Shauna had asked to help after someone had complained about Cat's penmanship one too many times in a session.

The ideas flowed for a while and soon, they slowed down and Shauna ripped the flip chart off to a second one where most of the ideas were already written down. "As you can see, a lot of the groundwork on these questions has already been done, so Shauna will put an x by the ones that were brought up in this brainstorming. Then we'll vote on the order. Most votes goes first. And if there's something you think of that's not on the list, let me know. We might have time to discuss or it might be covered under one of our other sessions."

Piper raised her hand. "So this is from other groups? Did the questions change from fiction to non-fiction retreats like ours?"

"Good question. Yes, this is the list from both fiction and non-fiction retreats. Maybe since I'm a fiction author, you all don't ask me the questions you'd ask a non-fiction author. Mostly, the process of getting published is the same, and that's our main goal, right? To get our words out to others to read?" Cat glanced at Shauna who nodded. "Okay, the topics with lines in front are the things you brought up that you wanted to talk about. There were two new items, congrats. Shauna added them to the list. Now, we'll vote on what order we want these. I believe we can get through most of them in one sitting, but if you have a favorite that doesn't get talked about today, I'd be glad to give you some time on Thursday. It's our no-planned-session day. Raise your hand if you really want to talk about a subject and we'll count. The topics with the most hands, go first. The first topic, Do I Need an Agent. Hands?"

They went through the list and as they did, other items were written down and some clarified and combined. After ten minutes, they had a topic list for Cat to work from. Shauna excused herself and the session got started. By the time it was over, Cat had talked about or touched on all the questions listed on the flow chart. She glanced at her watch. "And that's time. We went ten minutes over but covered all the questions. Now, remember, we'll get together again on Friday night to talk about the session and what worked and what your homework is going to be when you leave. But I'm here if you want to chat about anything writing related. Just let me know."

She turned around and saw Uncle Pete in the lobby area watching her. Shauna must have left the door to the living room open as she left. He was sitting in the little conversation grouping she'd set up by the hallway fireplace. She turned back to the group, but people were getting up and leaving. "Tomorrow is totally on your own, but if you want to snowshoe again tomorrow afternoon, let Seth know and he'll get you a guide. I'm going to be in my office, unless you want to chat more. Just let me know."

She waited for the group to leave, then met Uncle Pete by the fireplace. She sank into the other chair and sighed. "So what's going on?"

"I got the autopsy back and got some unexpected results. Jewel was ten weeks' pregnant. They're trying to run DNA on the baby, but I'm not sure it will give us much." He held his hat in his hand and Cat could see the fatigue on her uncle's face.

"Are you okay?" She reached over and rubbed his arm.

He nodded, not meeting her gaze. "Sometimes, it's just a lot. Shirley has been hounding me for months to think about announcing a retirement date. With this last death, killing a pregnant woman, what is the world coming to?"

She rubbed his arm. Uncle Pete had been in law enforcement for his entire career. He'd seen a lot but Jewel's death was really affecting him.

"I didn't think Jewel was seeing anyone. She said she'd been having an affair with Tom Cook and was still upset about his death, but if so, how did she get pregnant. He died several years ago."

Uncle Pete sat up and put his hat back on. "I think I need to look into Miss Jewel's background. Maybe the baby daddy didn't want a kid?"

"Especially if she was still hung up on a dead guy," Cat added as she walked her uncle out to the reception area. "Anyway, did you talk to Shirley?"

"I don't think she saw me sitting here. She went straight into the kitchen." He shook his head. "She's not happy with me, but what can I do? I have a murder investigation. I can't just ignore that and go sit in the hot springs with her for the afternoon. Even though I'd love to."

Cat put a hand on her uncle's arm. "We'll keep her busy here. What do you need from me?"

"Just stay out of my investigation, please. I don't need a band of Nancy Drew's messing up my crime scene." He tapped on her nose. "Oh, don't look so innocent. I'm sure you're all dying to help me figure out who killed one of your own. Writers and the Mafia, you both must share the same code."

"We're not that bad," Cat reminded him as she walked him to the door. "Besides, you love us. Me, Shirley, Shauna – we're all writers and you love all of us."

"Thank goodness I have Seth around to keep you all corralled or you'd probably paint a private investigation sign on the door and start messing with my crime clues." He paused at the door.

"Don't be silly. You have to have a license in Colorado to be a private investigator. Maybe we could have a Murders R Us shop where we could just help family members figure out what happened with their loved ones." Cat kissed him on the cheek.

"You are a pain in my side, Catherine Latimer." He squeezed her arms. "Just stay safe, please?"

"Of course. Oh, random question, is the Cook's cabin cleared? Linda had some things she needed to pick up from there."

He paused on the sidewalk. "I'm done with the cabin. Just don't make it a group field trip if you can help yourself."

Shauna met her at the front door after Uncle Pete had left. "Everything okay?"

Cat nodded and came inside. "It's too cold to be outside without a coat. I think I'm going with Seth to the Cook's cabin tomorrow. Anything you need from me that would keep me here?"

"No, unless one of your writers wants a question answered from today's lecture. I know you set yourself up as available to talk tomorrow too. You always do." Shauna walked with her to the kitchen. "Come in and tell me what your uncle told you. I offered him lunch, but he even refused coffee. He said he was just here to chat with you for a second, then he had to leave. I think he and Shirley are fighting."

"They are so cute together. I hope he doesn't blow it." Cat grabbed a bottle of water out of the fridge and sat down at the table. "Mom said this is the longest he's been in a real relationship for years. She met her at Christmas when Uncle Pete and Shirley went down to have dinner with the folks."

"You and Seth should have gone too." Shauna turned on the

teapot and set up her cup. "I could have survived by myself for a week."

"It wasn't just that. Seth and I, well, we're still tiptoeing around each other. The counseling isn't helping. Anytime we disagree, she sides with him. I want to ask her if she wants me to leave them alone."

"Cat, you can't be jealous of your therapist." Shauna poured the hot water over her teabag and sat down at the table. "Is this why you've been so quiet about your sessions? I thought it was because Seth wanted to keep that part of your lives just between the two of you. We live so close together, I just assumed."

"No, it's not that. Seth loves you to death, you know that. I just don't know how to handle this woman telling me everything I'm doing wrong. It's not all my fault, right?" Cat stood and grabbed a handful of tissues. "Now I'm crying. I never cry. Especially not on retreat week."

"Cat, you need to tell Seth how you feel about your therapist. That counseling isn't being helpful." Shauna stood and put her arm around her friend. "He loves you. You love him. You just hit a bad spot."

"I'll talk to him tomorrow on the way to the cabin." Cat dried her eyes. "Hopefully, he feels the same way. I'm not sure I can do another six months with this woman."

Cat felt better as she headed upstairs to put the talk, notes, and flipcharts in what she called her pending file. She'd update any information she needed to in the working file for the talk, making notes about who had attended this time. She hadn't been lying when she said most of the questions she got during retreats were the same. She'd expected more from her reunion group, but they'd just expanded on the questions already in the file. She'd talk with them again before they left. Cat wanted to make sure that a reunion group got what they needed out of the session. If not, there was no need to change the program. She'd just add more new attendees to the monthly session.

Her mind was still on Seth and their counseling sessions. Would he want to continue them? They'd been her idea in the first place, but right now, she felt like she was the only one making any changes. Maybe Seth was perfect in Dr. Hollis's eyes but for a completely different reason. Cat wondered if it was normal for someone to be jealous of their counselor.

Even if that was true, she didn't want Dr. Kristin Hollis in the middle of her relationship with Seth. Not anymore. Hopefully, Seth felt the same way. She'd talk with him on the way to the cabin tomorrow. Kill two birds with one stone.

Cat groaned. She even knew that sounded bad.

She sat at her computer and opened the word file she'd been working in that morning. But for some reason, she couldn't focus on the story. Finally, after playing around on the internet for over an hour, she went downstairs and popped into the kitchen. No one was there. She wrote a note, a habit that they'd all gotten into since the house was so big and they wanted to make sure someone knew if Seth was on the roof, or if Shauna had headed off for a ride on Snow. Cat wasn't sure where she was heading, so she said she was walking into town and would be back by dinner.

The temperature at night wasn't appropriate walking weather, so she planned on being back before the sun set and the winter cold turned the melted snow on the sidewalks icy. She bundled into her parka and pulled on a cap and gloves. She needed to think about where she was in the story and push out of her brain ideas of how to solve Jewel's murder.

Although if her uncle was going to blame Linda for this, all bets were off. She wasn't going to let her friend who had been through so much with her husband's death be accused of killing a woman who had either been lying about being in love with Tom Cook or had had the longest pregnancy in history. Of course, she could have had a relationship after Tom died with someone else, but from what she'd told Cat, she didn't think so.

The cold air was freezing her cheeks so she wrapped the scarf

Shauna had made and given her for Christmas around her face. Now, her breath was going out warm and then turning cold when she inhaled.

She wondered if Jewel had a copy of her book on her laptop. Had Shauna already packed everything up? If so, would Uncle Pete even let her read the woman's book? Maybe there were clues there that would give Cat an estimation of the affair's timeline. Maybe Linda would look at it and compare her knowledge of Tom's calendar with Jewel's?

She walked past Mrs. Rice's dark house. Soon her neighbor would be home from her cruise and watching Cat as she walked by her house from the large picture windows in the front room. The wind picked up and Cat shoved her hands deeper into her pockets. The sidewalks went from clear to snowy as soon as she passed Mrs. Rice's fence.

She slowed her walking to make sure she didn't slip or hit some black ice under the snow cover. She knew when she hit Dante's property because the sidewalks were free of any snow or ice. Even if the now mob boss was in Chicago handling business, his Colorado home was well tended. *It must be nice to have money and people to support you.*

Cat shook the envy away. She could have had more money out of Michael's inheritance, but she worried about how he'd come by it and if someone would come after it later. Dante had assured her that she'd be safe, but stuff happened. And people died.

When she looked up, she'd reached the school and the English department. The dean had made a Tom Cook memorial exhibit on the first floor. Of course, Tom and really, Linda, had donated a lot of money to the department, especially to support Aspen Hill's kids who wanted to attend college. Like the situation Cat had been in so many years ago. If she ever became wealthy through the books, she would do the same. But maybe she'd share some of the money with a college or two in Denver. And away from Covington.

Wishes and horses. Cat pulled open the building's door and

stepped into the warm lobby area. The Cook exhibit was to her left and a work study student sat at a desk by the entrance. She saw Cat approach and held out a clipboard. "Sign your name here. When you leave, there will be a box for your headphones. Just put them in the box and you're free to go. Each headphone is numbered, and we match them up at the end of the day, so don't get any ideas about taking one home."

Cat signed and reached for the headphones that the girl held out. "I'll remember to drop them before I leave. Do you have a lot of thieves around here?"

The girl shook her head. "I've never had a pair go missing. But I've been told I have to tell everyone the same thing because if I just picked random people to tell, I might be unconsciously profiling."

"Sounds like a good policy." Cat put the headphones on and turned on the recording before stepping into the exhibit.

For the next hour, she learned a lot about Tom Cook, the man and the manuscripts. The most interesting thing she learned about Tom today, she thought as she left the exhibit and left her headphones in the box by the exit door was about his younger brother who was also an English teacher and had published a book. Not that it took off, but published was published. And Boyd Cook looked a lot like his older brother.

Cat hurried back to the house to do some research before dinner. Maybe there was an explanation to why Jewel had thought she was having an affair with Tom.

CHAPTER

NINE

T hursday was a free day for the writers, and no one had asked Cat for any one-on-one time to talk. Yet. So at breakfast, she waited for Seth to show up and asked if she could go with him to Tom and Linda's cabin.

Seth glanced at Shauna. "Are you okay with being here alone with Cat's writer friends?"

"As long as the two of you don't disappear until Monday, yes, I can handle being by myself for a few hours." Shauna set a stack of pancakes in front of Seth. "What are you looking for, Miss Curious Cat?"

"Why do you think," Cat started then shook her head. "Never mind, you're right. I need to see where Jewel was killed. Why was she going there? And was she meeting someone? Jewel was adamant that she had to be here in this session. We didn't tell anyone we were doing the reunion section in January. She didn't know Linda would be here."

Shauna sat down at the table with a cup of coffee. "I thought that was odd too. Now, I understood her reasoning. Sometimes jobs are less than happy when you take off time. But I felt like there was more to the story. Something she wasn't telling us."

"You can't think that Jewel thought Tom Cook was still alive." Seth looked from Cat to Shauna. "Seriously?"

"I don't know. Uncle Pete let slip that Jewel was pregnant when she died. What if she *thought* she was the only one who knew Tom Cook was alive?" Cat looked at her friends. "Am I seeing zebras?"

Seeing zebras was the trio's code for taking a simple answer and looking for a more complicated, less likely answer. Seth and Shauna paused and Cat could see the look pass between the two of them. "You think I'm going off the deep end, don't you?"

Shauna reached for her hand. "I wouldn't say that, but it's kind of farfetched."

Cat banged her head against the table. "Fine, I'll look for horses. Besides, Uncle Pete will probably have this case tied up today. You know he likes having time with Shirley when she comes to town."

She also knew that her uncle wouldn't shortchange the investigation just because he had company in town. Cat decided to let this sleeping dog lie and change the subject. "Anyway, what time do you think you're heading out to the cabin?"

"Linda already told me she's not coming. She left me a list." Seth glanced at his watch. "So we can leave around ten if that works. I've got some things to get done and I'll need to separate Mr. Peeps and Sam into different rooms. He doesn't like that cat much. Which is weird since he loves Angelica."

"Sam's smart and he knows that it's Mrs. Rice's cat." She stood and put her plate in the sink. "Okay, I'm going upstairs to try to write a bit. Come get me when you're ready."

"Sounds like we're playing hooky from school." Seth grinned. "We should have a code word and you shouldn't open your office door to anyone who doesn't know it."

"Code knock. That way I don't let the visitor know I'm there unless it's you. It would ruin my hiding place." Cat gave Seth a kiss and headed to the stairwell. She needed to stop thinking about Jewel and focus on her manuscript.

When Seth came to get her, he'd already packed her snowshoes and snowsuit in the SUV. They had hot cocoa in a thermos along with sandwiches and soups for lunch. He started the engine. "Shauna thought we might need some sustenance. I think she's expecting us to get snowed in up there for a few days."

"This might be her evil plan to take over the writers' retreats. She's already running the nightly word sprints." Cat buckled in and set her tote on the floor. "I guess we'll just have to trust her."

"You brought her back from California. I think if we can't, this is on your head." Seth pulled the car out on the road. "So how are you feeling about things."

"About us, you mean." Cat took his free hand in hers. "Seth, I want to ask you something."

"You're asking if you can ask? Isn't that redundant?"

She shook her head. "Technically, I didn't ask you, I told you that I wanted to ask you something. There's a difference."

"Slight but go ahead." Seth was clearly amused by her word play. That hadn't been her intention.

"I don't want to see Dr. Hollis anymore." She didn't look at him but she didn't let go of his hand, either.

"Thank goodness. I thought something was really wrong." Seth turned onto the highway and took the road that went out of town to the left. "I think that's an excellent idea. Do we get another therapist or just work on our relationship the old fashion way by fighting it out?"

"I don't want another therapist," Cat admitted.

"Okay, but when we fight, you have to use your words and not just disappear into your books or your head. That's my one condition." He stopped at a light. "Well, that and I need to know that you forgive me for taking off for that last mission. I thought with that money, we'd be set for life. I didn't consider what might happen to me and what that might do to you. I just want us to be happy again."

"I do forgive you. I should have told you how I felt before you left. I was scared that you wouldn't come home." Cat wiped the back of her hand across her cheek bones. "I do tend to shut down during fights. You know it's all or nothing with me."

"I should have been more open and made it an 'us' decision. You just have so much on your plate, with the retreat and the books. I thought I could bring more into the relationship. Instead, I messed us up." Seth pulled the SUV into the trailhead parking for the cabin access. He pulled her closer and kissed her. "I promise no more 'Me Tarzan, You Jane' boneheaded moves. At least for a while."

Cat giggled as they got out of the vehicle. "You're just built that way, Seth. And it's one of the reasons I love you."

"So you like the image? I'll have to remember that for the next costume party after my leg heals up more. I don't think I'll be swinging from trees for a while." He glanced around the trailhead. "I need to chat with Pete about his guys making a mess up here. There's trash all over."

"I'll clean it up while you're getting our equipment ready." Cat grabbed a bag out of the travel case they always kept in the vehicles. Especially in winter. You never knew what the mountain roads could bring. She picked up coffee cups, energy drink cans, and then she found some white paper that was on a rock. It had probably been covered after the last snowfall, but the rock and sun had generated enough heat to melt the snow and dry the paper.

She glanced at it, then realized, it was a plane ticket. Most people did tickets on their phone. At least she did. One less thing to carry around. This had probably been here a while, but the paper didn't seem to have degraded at all. She read the flight information. Southwest from Connecticut to Denver with a stopover in St. Louis. For last week. But she couldn't read the year.

The ticket could have been anyone's. She tried to read the name, but it had been blurred by the water damage.

"We're ready to go. You just have to climb into your snowsuit,"

Seth stepped behind her, reaching for the bag. "We can throw this in the back."

"Seth, I might have found something." She showed him the ticket.

"There's a lot of people up here in the winter, Cat." He pulled out his phone. "I have some service. Hold it against your coat for contrast and I'll send it to Pete."

They managed to get a fairly clear picture of the ticket. Cat walked over and put it in a treat baggie to keep the ticket separate from the trash. "I'll get ready to go unless you think we need to take that to Uncle Pete now."

Seth took the baggie and put it into the glove box between the two front seats. "Let's get this trip up to the cabin done. We'll drop the ticket off if he needs it on the way back to the house. There's a storm coming in tonight and I don't want to disappoint Linda."

"Give me a second and I'll be ready." Cat knew that finding the ticket was chance, and it might not even mean anything. She decided to let her uncle make that decision. She was heading to a murder scene, and she needed her wits about her.

The walk to the cabin was beautiful. The trail was the road to the cabins, but since it had several feet of snow hiding the gravel, they had to be careful near the edges. The trail seemed to climb upward, then settle for a bit, then another climb. Cat was breathing hard when Seth pointed to a clearing between two trees.

"That's the driveway to the cabin. We're almost there." He peered at her through his goggles. "Are you okay or do you need a break?"

She shook her head. "I'm good. How's your leg?"

"Burning like a ..." He groaned as he rubbed the snowsuit on his thigh. "Anyway, let's just say I won't be doing anything strenuous for a few days. We might have snowy sidewalks tomorrow."

"I'll clear them." She flashed him a grin. "I know where the keys to the 4wheeler are."

Seth had put a snowblade on the ATV last year and loved taking it out to clear the new snow off the concrete. "We'll see. I might not need any help. Driving the ATV isn't the problem. It's the detail work."

She glanced up at the driveway. It wasn't a big hill, but it seemed like it from where they stood. "Have you rested enough?"

"I didn't stop for me," Seth clarified. He narrowed his eyes when he saw her grin. "You're a brat."

"And you love me." Cat adjusted her poles and nodded. "Let's see what shape they left the cabin in. We might have to hire someone to come clean when the roads clear. I don't think you can get a disaster cleaner who snowshoes into their job sites."

"It's Colorado, so who knows," Seth said as he followed her. "If it's bad, I'll check with Pete and then let Linda know what the options are."

"Fingers crossed it's not like the trailhead." Cat hoped that the emergency crew hadn't made that mess. Maybe it was from other snowshoers.

As they crested the hill, she saw the cabin. The sun was shining on the rooftop and the surrounding area. The cabin looked magical. Except for the snowshoes sitting out front. They had already been snowed on again.

"Don't let me forget to grab those as we're leaving. The rental company is going to charge us enough to replace Jewel's snowsuit. At least we can give them back the snowshoes." Seth dug in his pocket for the keys. "My backpack has room but we're going to have to move some of the stuff over to yours for the trip down."

"I wondered why I was carrying an empty backpack. Linda must have given you a list of stuff she wants." Cat followed him into the cabin. She glanced around. "It looks normal. Dusty and the floor's a mess, but not the crime scene mess I expected."

"She was hit in the head with a fireplace poker. I don't think she bled or at least not from the wound." Seth opened the heavy curtains so they could see the cabin better. "Here's a list of the books that Linda is looking for. I guess they're missing from her home library, and she wanted to collect them. She said she was thinking about selling the cabin."

Cat glanced around and found a built-in bookcase that covered one wall. "It's a beautiful cabin."

Seth sighed as he looked around. "I've always wanted one of these. Nothing too big, just enough to hang out in the summer. The river is walking distance from here and you could probably hike for miles."

"We live close enough that we can hike or fish on day trips and still be home at night." Cat had never seen the need for a mountain cabin, especially since Aspen Hills was surrounded by mountains.

He chuckled as he went up the stairs to check the loft bedroom. "It's not the same, Cat."

She shrugged. Maybe it was a man thing. Living life in a small cabin without internet or even electricity. She got out her phone and took pictures of the cabin. Seth was right, the floor was dirty and there were medical gloves, tubes and other supplies scattered on the floor. She grabbed another bag out of her pocket and gathered up the debris. At least Linda wouldn't need to see evidence of Jewel dying here. She got down on her hands and knees and scanned the floor. As she glanced around for more trash, she saw something white under the couch. Pulling it out, she realized it was a folded sheet of paper.

Opening it, she found directions to the cabin. This must have been how Jewel found the place. Which meant if she had been meeting someone for an affair, it hadn't been here. The directions looked like they were part of an email. The end was a salutation, "See you on Sunday. We'll make plans for the week then. TC"

Cat stuck the note into her pocket. How come Uncle Pete's officers hadn't found it? She stood and slowly turned around the cabin. Clearly Jewel had thought she was meeting someone here. And she'd been seeing someone because of the pregnancy.

The fireplace had ashes in the grate. Had Jewel made a fire or had someone been here waiting for her. No wonder her uncle was looking at Linda. Shirley couldn't find her that day until after Jewel was killed. Had she waited to meet up with someone to set her alibi?

Cat shook her head. That didn't make sense since Linda hadn't known that Shauna had asked Shirley to go to the cabin with her. She'd left before Shauna could tell her.

She glanced at the list of books and went over to the bookshelf. She found most of the items on the list, except for *Alice in Wonderland*. Seth was coming down the stairs with a bag in his hand. "Did you find any books up there?"

He shook his head. "I went through the nightstands. Linda thought she left a bracelet up here. It was in one of the drawers. It's really nice, probably worth some money. And she asked for any journals that Tom had left here. I found two. He's got a ton of nice winter clothes up here. She's got fewer, but there all top outdoor brands."

"I'm missing only one book off the list. *Alice in Wonderland*." She walked around the small cabin, opening cabinets and drawers and checking under the sofa cushions. "I don't see it here."

"Maybe he gave it away to a kid," Seth said as he glanced at his watch. "We need to finish this up. Do you want cocoa or water with your protein bar?"

"Cocoa please. The cabin is cold. Did you see that there was a fire lit?"

He glanced over as he emptied his bag, tossing Cat one of the bars. He set the thermos's on the table. "The guys might have lit one to warm up the place as they were working here."

"I don't think so." Cat unwrapped her bar and quickly ate it. She was hungrier that she'd thought. "The soups in the car?"

"Yep. I thought we'd eat at the trailhead," he handed her cocoa. "This is just a snack to keep you from collapsing on the way back."

"You're thoughtful that way." She leaned against the wall, looking at the cabin. "I found a sheet with directions to the cabin."

He stared at her, then shook his head. "You're going to get all your uncle's employees fired for not doing their jobs."

"Shoddy workmanship is not my problem," she pointed to the

living room. "I was cleaning up the medical supplies and that paper was under the couch. I don't think Jewel has been here before."

"If she was having an affair with him, don't you think they'd use his cabin?" Seth shook his head. "I don't like speaking ill of the dead, but it doesn't make sense. Jewel said this was the first time been in the Denver area when I picked everyone up on Saturday."

"There's a lot about this whole thing that doesn't make sense," Cat shivered, feeling the chill of the cabin even through the heavy snowsuit she wore. "She told someone, Piper, I think that she'd had a lay over in Denver."

"Finish your cocoa and let's get out of here." Seth glanced through the window. "I don't want to get stuck here."

"Not that it wouldn't be a lovely escape," Cat finished her cocoa. They had responsibilities at home and Jewel's killer was still at large. Being snowed in sounded like the break they needed soon. Just not today.

CHAPTER

TEN

Uncle Pete was out of the police station when Cat and Seth stopped to drop off the two papers they'd found. They also left the sacks of trash they collected, just in case they'd missed something as they were collecting. The new receptionist frowned when Seth put the sacks on the floor in Pete's office. "I'm not sure he'll appreciate that."

"Well, it's better than someone having to go through the dumpster if we drop it off in the back," Cat pointed out.

The woman, Amanda Foss, from her nametag nodded. "I guess. This job is really weird at times."

"I don't think we've met yet," Cat took off her glove and reached out her hand. "I'm Cat Latimer, I'm Pete's niece."

"Oh, I know all about you. Pete's got me reading your books. I get a lot of down time here, so I have lots of free time. When my work is done, I'm just hanging out waiting for calls or visitors. Like you, bringing in sacks of trash." Amanda made a face at the office.

Cat laughed as they moved back into the hallway. "One man's trash, so to speak."

"I guess. It was nice to meet you." The phone rang and Amanda

90

stepped back behind her desk. "Aspen Hills Police Department, this is Amanda. May I help you?"

As Cat and Seth walked out of the building and back to the car, he looked at her. "She seems nice."

"Nice and not in love with my uncle," Cat opened the door and climbed in. "Two new requirements for his administrative assistant position."

When Seth got in on the driver's side, he looked at her. "Do you think he'll really retire? Who would take his place?"

"I don't know. But I think Shirley's getting tired of waiting for him. Maybe we can talk on Sunday about their future plans." Cat put on her seatbelt.

"Sure, but you start the conversation. I don't want to be the one to start a fight between them on the night before Shirley's going home to Alaska." Seth started the engine and turned toward her. "We're good, the two of us, then? Should I call and cancel Monday's appointment?"

Cat smiled and squeezed his hand. "We're more than good. But let me cancel the appointment."

"Don't break our therapist's heart," Seth grinned as he checked for traffic as he pulled out.

"I'll be as nice to her as she's been to me," Cat replied as she watched the snow-covered streets of downtown Aspen Hills. The stores were open, but there weren't a lot of people walking around. Not like there would be during summer. Now, people ran from the car to the shop and back to stay warm.

Winter in Colorado took some getting used to. Especially for newcomers.

When they got back to the house, the writers were scattered. Deek and Andi were in the dining room, filling plates with snacks.

"Hey, it's our fearless leader. Where did you and your dude run off to this morning? Shauna's being really tight lipped about your absence. Were you investigating Jewel's murder?" Deek leaned against the table and watched as Cat took off her snowsuit and hung it from a hook on the wall. She slipped into booties that she'd left there that morning.

"We had an errand to run." Cat pulled on a hoodie.

Deek watched her but didn't say anything.

"Fine, we went up to the cabin for Linda. How did you know?" Cat joined them in the dining room and poured herself a cup of coffee. She sat at the table with a brownie. Deek and Andi joined her at the table.

Deek grinned. "My boss, Jill, she gets the same look after she's been out investigating. Or if I catch her before she leaves. She doesn't meet my eyes when she talks to me. She doesn't really lie, she just, like you did, tells partial truths. So did you find anything?"

"Kind of. Maybe." She looked at Deek and Andi. "Did Jewel say anything about being here before? Or it being her first time in Colorado?"

"Not to me," Deek glanced at Andi. "You two talked after Seth picked us up at the airport. Did she tell you anything like that?"

Andi nodded. "She was so excited to be here. She said that this was her first trip to Colorado, but it wouldn't be her last. I figured she was talking about the snow because we talked about the snow-shoeing adventure the next day. She pulled up a map and showed me our trail."

"Jewel had a trail map of the area around Aspen Hills?" Cat asked. "Did she say where she got it?"

"Yes. She said she had to order it from the forest service a few months ago." Andi looked up as Linda came into the room. "Hey Linda, how's the writing going?"

Linda shrugged as she came into the dining room. "Well, since I could have gotten coffee and cookies in the room where I'm writing and I chose instead to walk down a flight of stairs to find people, that should tell you something."

Deek laughed and pulled out a chair. "Grab your poison and sit with us. We're all feeling the burn out of the day. Although I have to say, I'm making great progress on this new story. I love the making stuff up part so the first book goes fast. It's the second book where I'm questioning whose eyes were brown or did I ever even describe them in the first place?"

"The joy of writing a series," Linda responded as she put cookies on a plate and poured herself a cup of coffee. "Tom used to complain all the time about that. He always said he was going to write a series bible, but then he'd get lost in the story. He loved telling stories."

"Are you having trouble writing?" Cat asked as Linda sat down. "Too many people around?"

Linda pointed to her head. "Too many memories. I'll be writing about something then go off on a tangent about how he loved collecting old books, especially those that held meaning for him from childhood."

"Oh," Cat realized why she'd collected so many children's books this morning at the cabin. "Good news, Seth and I ran to the cabin and I got all but one of the books from the list you gave him."

Linda brightened at the news. "I'm so glad. I had wanted to gift some of the books to Tom's niece this Christmas but then I realized they weren't in our home library. I bought her new copies of the books, but I'd love to give her the rarer versions that Tom collected for when she's older and she'll appreciate the books. What book was missing?"

"*Alice in Wonderland*. We looked in cupboards and closets and under the sofa cushions, even." Cat sipped her coffee. She was almost thawed out from their morning adventure.

"Well, it might have gotten lost. Which is too bad. Tom paid quite a sum for that book. I bet whoever has it now is totally unaware of its value." She wrapped the cookies in a napkin. "Where are the books you found? I'll get them ready and ship them home tomorrow after our trip to the bookstore. I know I'll find something I can't live without when I'm there. I always do."

Cat walked her over to the bench where she'd left the backpack. "If I'd known they were expensive, I would have wrapped them."

"Oh, they'll be fine. Do you mind if I use this backpack to take them up to my room?" Linda opened the bag and smiled as she thumbed through the books. "Tom was so excited when he found this copy of *A Wrinkle in Time*. He said he had one with this exact cover as a kid."

Cat watched as Linda put the bag over her shoulder and headed to the west wing.

Seth came in the front door with his backpack and the cooler that had held their lunches. He saw Cat watching Linda and put the cooler on the floor. "Everything okay?"

"Yeah, she just misses Tom I think." She nodded toward the hallway. "You catch up with her with the rest of the books and I'll take this into the kitchen."

"Are you sure?" He adjusted the backpack. "I can take the cooler to the kitchen door for you."

"Knock it off, strongman. I'm perfectly capable of carrying the almost empty cooler a few feet." She grabbed the cooler and followed him down the hallway. As she turned to open the door by backing in, she smiled at Seth. "Thanks for the outing. It was a great day."

"It was, wasn't it." He headed up the set of stairs that went to the second floor of the west wing. Seth's apartment took up the first floor of the wing. Someday, that area would be hers and Seth's home. Except she'd still keep her office in the other wing. Maybe. She hadn't thought that far ahead of just today's conversation.

Shauna was in the kitchen doing dishes as she came into the room. "Hey, when did you get back?"

"Just now. Seth's taking Linda's stuff up to her room, so I told him I'd bring this in. Do you want me to clean it out?" Cat opened the lid to the cooler and looked inside. There were four dirty thermoses and a few empty baggies, but not much else. She took the thermoses over to the sink.

"Just leave it there and I'll wash it down before I take it downstairs to put in storage." Shauna was watching out the window. "Did you have a good talk?"

"We had the best talk." Cat threw away the baggies and then

closed the cooler top. "We're done with therapy. Ding, dong, the wicked therapist is dead."

"I'm not sure that's a very mature attitude." Shauna laughed as she rinsed a bowl. "But I know that you didn't trust her so that can't be helpful in therapy."

"I just needed to understand why he left. And let him know that he hurt my feelings." Cat grabbed a soda from the fridge.

"Did he get anything from you?" Shauna asked.

"You sound like you've done this therapy thing before," Cat responded. "Yes, I told him that I'd trust him and I'd tell him when he upsets me rather than hide behind my books."

"Wow, you did have a great session. Without your therapist." Shauna took her cloth and went over to the counter to wash the cooler." She met Cat's gaze. "How'd your secret mission go? Did you find anything?"

"A couple of things that may or may not be part of the investigation. We dropped them off with Uncle Pete." Cat sipped her soda.

"I bet he loved that." Shauna said, dryly.

"He wasn't there, so the lecture will come later." Cat stood. "I'm running upstairs to work for a few hours. I'll see you at dinner?"

"Actually, I'll have a casserole ready at six but I'm not eating with you guys," Shauna paused. "Can you run the Night Games tonight? I have an appointment."

"At night? An appointment or a date?" Cat leaned against the doorway and watched her.

"A dinner," Shauna clarified. "And that's all I'm going to tell you."

AFTER DINNER, Cat was in the living room, waiting for the writers to get back from their dinner in town. She wondered if they should start doing a second meal here at the house, at least in the winter months. Getting to the local restaurants wasn't an issue when the roads weren't covered with snow like they are now.

Linda Cook came into the living room first. She was shaking. "I can't believe what I just saw."

"Linda, are you okay?" Cat helped her onto the couch. "What happened?"

She put her hands over her face. "I just think it's Aspen Hills. Maybe this place just has too many memories for me."

"Did you run into an old friend?" Cat was worried about Linda. She was writing a book about her husband who was killed here in this house. Maybe having her here for a reunion session hadn't been the best idea.

"No. It's nothing," Linda sat up but even then, she had her arms wrapped around herself. "I left the Diner early. The other writers like to sit and chat after they eat, and I wasn't feeling it, not today. Not after getting the mementos from the cabin. I decided to walk down Main Street. Some of the Christmas displays are still up and a lot of the lights. I love walking through town. The lights make it look like a village at the North Pole. Anyway, I turned the corner and a man walked out of a bar. He got into a car and then left. Cat, I would have sworn that it was Tom getting into that car."

"Tom?" Cat didn't like where this was going.

"Yes Tom. I know how it sounds. I wanted to run after the car, but I was frozen solid. Literally and figuratively." Linda glanced over her shoulder as the others came into the room. She dropped her voice. "Cat, I swear it was like that big time travel book that had been made into a series. He stepped out of the Old Mill and then into the car. Like it was choreographed for just one person to see. Me."

Linda excused herself to go get coffee and left the room. Deek came over to Cat, still watching her leave. "Do you think she'll be okay?"

"Linda's just had an emotional day." Cat lied but she wasn't sure on what she should say. "Deek, do you want to lead this session of Night Games?"

"Is snow white?" Deek grinned. "Don't answer that. Yes, I'd love to lead tonight's session unless there's something you're not telling me and you're keeping me from going all superhero on someone."

Cat wanted to investigate. To figure out who had killed Jewel, but all her leads had disappeared. The only thing she could think of was to look at Jewel herself. Maybe that would give her some clarity. She'd had two conversations with the woman and Cat hadn't reached out for more. Mostly because she'd been mean to Linda.

Maybe by looking into Jewel's history and talking to people who'd known her before, maybe that would fill in some of these gaps. She could start with the group. "I do need to talk to everyone first."

"So you *are* going off to investigate." Deek held out a hand. "I'm used to my boss taking Off like this, so don't worry about me. I'll step in and do the grunt work."

"Oh, I didn't want you to feel obligated. I can run the Night Games." Cat froze, realizing that she may have gone too far.

"Cat, I love running these things. I have two writing groups that I lead at home. It's not an obligation. I learn as much as the others. I just like having a little bit of order in the process. So, I volunteer before anyone who would drive me crazy raises their hands. You'd think, for a bunch of organizational experts, these people would be better at time management." He sat down in the circle, pulling out his laptop and putting it on the coffee table. "If you want to get this discussion done before Linda comes back, I suggest you start now."

Cat squeezed Deek's shoulder and stepped up to the podium. She had a pen and a notebook always available for anyone to use, so she turned it to a fresh page. "Hey gang, I've got some questions. You may have already told my uncle but humor me. Who talked to Jewel before she died?"

Piper, Andi, and Ryan raised their hands.

"Piper, you and she chatted while you snowshoed, any other time?" Cat wrote down the three names.

"I tried to talk with her at breakfast that morning, but she got her food and went to her room. She kept looking at her phone, like she was expecting a call." Piper shrugged. "I'm not very good at making friends, so I try to engage people quickly so maybe we could bond during the week. It's stupid, I know."

Andi put a hand on her arm. "It's not stupid. And you must put yourself out there with others. I thought you were just busy with your book. We can carve out some time to talk tomorrow if you want."

"Now I feel like I'm begging for time," Piper shrugged, "but I'll take it."

The group laughed and Cat was again struck by how the writers just seemed to know how to pull the group together. "Those were the only two times. Did she talk about her past or her regular life at all?"

Piper shook her head. "I learned more about her during her fight with Linda than I did all the time she was here."

"She stayed in her room a lot that first day," Andi agreed. "And she was always looking at her phone. Waiting for a call."

"Okay, Andi, what did you chat with Jewel about?" Cat wrote down cell phone numbers and wondered if Uncle Pete had gone down that path.

"The town. She was really interested in my time at Covington. How I got in. If I was a townie on scholarship." Andi rubbed her jeans with a finger. "Now that I think about it, she was really interested in the college. Like how many people were on scholarship. She said she looked up the college website and their admissions page was very clear that most of the admits were legacies, relatives of employees, or town kids. I guess I never thought about going anywhere else since my dad was a professor here."

Cat stopped writing. "She was focused on how you got into Covington?"

Andi nodded and Ryan held up a hand. "She asked me the same questions. Where I was from, what my parents did for a living, and under what category I was admitted under to Covington. I was confused by her question. I guess I thought she was talking about affirmative action policies, and it made me mad. Just because my mom has Japanese heritage doesn't mean that I got into school because my ethnicity put a thumb on the scale."

"I'm not sure that's what she was looking for," Cat admitted. She decided to jump into the unspoked question. "Ryan, were you on scholarship?"

He shook his head. "Kind of? My Uncle Joey went here years ago. He's married to my mom's sister. I guess I fell under the legacy rule but I had the grades. I was also admitted to Stanford, but it wasn't a free ride. My mom told me to not look a gift horse in the mouth. Especially if the offer came with a full scholarship."

"Did Covington recruit you?" Cat wondered if a lot of these kids didn't even know Covington's history. Even if they were counted as legacies in the financial aid department. Ryan apparently didn't know why his uncle had attended Covington.

"I didn't apply here. They said they got my name off the PSAT list. I did really well on that test." Ryan looked around the room. "What's so special about my financial aid packet?"

"Dude, you're so lucky. I have student loans and I went to a cheap school." Deek leaned back in his chair. "But I also spent the last ten years on campus. I didn't want to leave so my mom stopped financing my schooling and the financial aid ran out."

Cat heard the door open behind her, she turned and watched as Linda came into the room.

She looked at Cat. "Did I miss something?"

"We were just chatting about Covington. Well, with that, Deek's going to run your Night Games tonight." Cat took the notebook and headed up to her office. She needed to chat with Dante and see if Jewel had been researching Covington and not Tom Cook.

CHAPTER

ELEVEN

C at was in the kitchen the next morning when Shauna left the room to take a call. When she returned, she nodded to the door. "Cat, you have a visitor in the living room."

Cat topped off her coffee and nodded. Then she went to the living room and opened the pocket door. Dante Cornelio had gotten her text and had come to chat. "I hope Shauna got you coffee."

"Miss Shauna has been very welcoming. I have coffee and two cookies. I can't stay long. I'm heading back to Boston later today and need to finish up a few items before I go." He sat his cup on the coffee table. "It's good to see you, Catherine. Honestly, I was surprised to get your text last night. What's on your mind?"

"I know you probably already answered this for Uncle Pete but humor me." Cat realized she kept saying that as sat next to Dante, sitting her cup down next to his. "Was Jewel Doan's death due to something she was investigating for her book?"

His dark eyes flashed for a second and Cat wondered if he thought she'd asked him here for a personal reason, or, more likely, he might not appreciate the implication that his organization was to blame. Or would do that. But that was something he'd never say. "The families were not involved in any way in Ms. Doan's death. I'm not even sure we were aware of her investigations until after her death. At least the fact she was even writing a book was a surprise to me, and, Catherine, nothing is a surprise to me in regard to family business."

Cat tried to translate what he was telling her. Since Dante's promotion in his family business, he'd been more guarded and less forthcoming in his willingness to share information. The fact that Cat had told him that they'd never be more than friends probably hadn't helped their ability to have an open conversation.

"Jewel said she was having an affair with Tom Cook, but Linda says that's not true." Cat decided to be open with Dante. Maybe that would help him respond in kind.

"Often spouses are the last to know if their loved ones have moved on." He sipped his coffee, but locked gazes with her. "You are aware, more than most, that sometimes, even when a spouse thinks something, the truth is something far different."

Dante never spoke directly. And it drove her crazy. "You're saying Linda's fooling herself?"

He stared at her. "Sometimes it's easy to believe the worst. Why would anyone want to create a doubt in a widow's mind? I think it's cruel. Especially if it's not true."

Cat knew Dante was trying to tell her something important. The problem was she didn't know if it was aimed at Linda or at her own relationship with her deceased husband.

"If there's nothing else," Dante stood, dusting cookie crumbs from his black suit. "I need to finish up my errands."

"One more thing. I wanted to thank you for distributing Michael's estate. The library is excited about their donation." Cat grabbed his arm. "I appreciate your help with the distributions. I'm not sure I could have been as thoughtful in the gifts."

He pulled her into a brief, distant hug. When he let her go, he smiled. "Catherine, you are one of the most thoughtful people I know. It was a pleasure to help you distribute Michael's estate. He was my best friend. I hope I can call you a friend as well."

Cat watched as he pulled on his coat. This conversation was over. She wondered about the answers that she'd been given. One, Jewel's death wasn't because she was digging into the background of Covington College. Because if she had been killed by someone in the family to protect secrets, he would have known. And two, she thought Linda was right. Tom Cook hadn't had an affair with Jewel, at least. She walked Dante to the door. "So one more question, are you dating Shauna?"

He laughed as he reached for the door. "That, my friend, is a discussion you need to have with someone besides me."

Cat watched him walk to the waiting town car parked in front of her house. Dante Cornelio was a mystery man which made him attractive to women. She wasn't in love with him, but she cared about him. Mostly because he'd loved Michael as a brother. And because of that, he watched out for her.

Now that she knew what Dante knew, and Uncle Pete, it was time to look closer at Jewel. She went into the kitchen where she'd left her notebook and made notes about what she'd learned from Dante. Shauna came in from outside as she wrote. "Dante's gone."

"I wasn't asking," Shauna said as she took off her coat and boots. "I think we need to keep the cats in the house until spring. It's too cold out there."

"He wouldn't tell me if you two were dating." Cat didn't turn to look at her friend. "He said to ask you."

"And I've answered your question before. I am not in a romantic relationship with anyone, including Dante. Yes, we have had dinner several times and he has sent me flowers, but Cat, the man has baggage with a capital B. If it was only his attachment to you, I could work with that. But he has professional obligations that I can't get past."

"But you like him." Cat watched as Shauna sat at the table.

"I also liked the Hell's Angel Club President I was dating in California. That relationship almost got me killed when his former girlfriend decided I wasn't worthy." Shauna paused a minute then looked at Cat. "I'm attracted to dangerous and broken men. There should be a Bad Boys Anonymous club that I could join to get on a 12-step program. My next great love is going to be a normal, boy next door type who loves his mama and listens to country music. If he rides, that will be a bonus."

"Rides a horse, not a motorcycle?" Cat clarified.

"Yes, a horse. I could do with a white knight on a shiny steed." She glanced at the clock. "I need to get breakfast out to the kids. Are you writing this morning?"

"They have a trip to the bookstore at ten this morning. I thought I'd ride along." Cat stood and filled a carafe. "So I have a couple of hours to write before that. Thanks for talking Dante into coming by this morning."

"Are you kidding? I had to stop him from running over in the middle of dinner last night." Shauna put a basket of muffins on a tray. "He cares for you, Cat."

"I'm in love with Seth," Cat responded as she headed out of the kitchen.

THE GROUP WAS all waiting in the foyer when Cat came back downstairs. She'd grabbed a muffin when she was in the kitchen, so she called that breakfast. A lot of days she didn't even eat until lunch, so she wasn't starving when she came down, dressed in jeans and her Ugh boots to head to the bookstore.

"I'm so glad you're coming with us," Andi greeted her as she crossed the foyer. "My writing group is begging Tammy to have you come talk about your books."

"I need to schedule a visit. What days do you meet again?" Cat had a task of visiting the writer group on her list of to-dos for too long. "It's hard to get me out at night anymore. I feel like an old lady."

"You're just busy telling yourself stories," Deek corrected her. "A lot of my author friends say the same thing. Most of them are introverts so getting out in front of a group is like a vamp draining your life blood."

"That's a visual I'll use for my next author visit," Cat laughed as she pulled on her coat. "Not."

"Tom was the opposite. He was an extrovert, so he loved doing book tours. When he came home, he was filled with energy. He missed the people after a few months of straight writing." Linda had joined the group. "So he'd do at least one event every month. And he always agreed to interview his friends or a new author if he was asked by our local library. He liked being with other writers."

Cat liked listening to how others dealt with the event portion. And hearing that Tom loved it, but that he was an extrovert, made her feel better about her own mixed feelings. A horn beeped from outside. Seth had the van ready for them.

"Oh, one more thing, if you feel the need to buy several books and then realize your bags won't make weight for your airline, we'll be glad to handle shipping them to your home." Cat called as they walked out the door.

"You're the best," Wilder called back to her as he climbed into the van.

Cat got into the van last. She'd wanted to sit with one of the writers, but they'd all saved the shotgun seat for her. She glanced at Seth. "You realize we're the chaperones of the field trip."

"It's better than being this group's parental figures." He glanced in the rear view. "I'm not sure we could control them, and I know we couldn't afford the car insurance for this group."

"We hear you talking about us," Felix called to the front. "And just in case you're serious, I can get a U-Haul and be moved into my room permanently by the end of the month."

"You'd miss your wife and kids too much," Cat called back.

"Drat. The real world is messing with my fantasy writer world again," Felix responded. Then he held a closed fist to the heavens. "Curse you cruel world."

"Okay, theatrics aside, Tammy has a presentation, then you'll have thirty minutes to shop. Seth will bring the car back at eleven unless you all decide to have lunch first." Cat turned to look at the group, "Thoughts?"

"We'll do lunch and walk back," Deek glanced at the group to make sure no one was disagreeing. "I believe a few of us are hitting the library to work after lunch."

"That will work. If you want to leave your purchases at the bookstore, I'll be here at eleven to take any packages back to the house." Seth offered as he pulled in front of the bookstore. "And if you decide you need picked up at the library, or after dinner, just call the house. Seth's taxi service is available until nine. Then this van turns into a pumpkin."

"Dude, you're such a light weight," Deek playfully punched Seth in the arm.

Seth shook his head. "I just don't want any drunks throwing up in my van. I have to clean this thing you know."

Cat waited until everyone got out of the van and were heading to the bookstore. "I'll be here at eleven to pick up."

He leaned in and kissed her. "I know you will. That's why I'm coming back. I'm going to let Tammy deal with sending them their books."

"No, you're not. But it was sweet to say that." Cat got out of the van and shut the door. She watched as Seth drove away. She was really lucky to have a second chance with him. She frowned as she walked toward the bookstore door. Third chance. Or maybe even more since she knew they'd broken up in high school at least once. He was her rock. When she was drowning and when she was okay, he was always there.

"Cat, are you coming in?" Tammy held the bookstore door open and was watching her. "It's cold out here."

"I'm coming." Cat hurried into the bookstore. The Written Word was warm and smelled like coffee and books. Someone should turn this smell into perfume. Or maybe a cologne for men. That would attract women, much more than a clean minty smell. She took off her coat and hung it by the door. The group was gathered around the bookstore's author visit and events center. Many of them had coffee and were looking for a seat while others grabbed refreshments.

A table to the side of where Tammy would be speaking held a ton of goal setting books, planners, and a few of Cat's books. Cat opened the top one and realized it was new, she hadn't signed it yet. "Is this a reminder that I need to come in and sign books for you more often?"

"I'm all out of signed ones and I always sell your books to your retreat guests. Are you signing them later?" Tammy pulled a chair over to the table and handed Cat a pen.

"Actually, no. No one's asked me to sign a book to them." Cat shrugged off her coat and sat down. "You want me to sign all of these?"

"Please. I have your books on a local author shelf, and they sell like hotcakes. Especially to Covington English majors. I think they want to prove to themselves that they can make it in the real world." She moved a box toward Cat. "And when you're done, sign those and put them back in the box. That should keep me for a month or so."

Cat opened the first book and signed with a generic salutation over her name. "I'd complain about you making me work for a living, but I think you're my best bookstore."

"Whatever it takes," Tammy grinned as she headed to the front of the group. "Let's talk about bookstores."

As Cat signed the books, she listened to Tammy talk about the state of the independent bookstore and what authors can do to make sure their books are carried on shelves. A few minutes later, Tammy asked Deek to talk about his job working at a bookstore and setting up author visits.

"The one thing that authors tell me is that their newsletters sell books. So stealing that idea, I have a newsletter for the bookstore too. I know some of the stores share newsletter information they get from publishers, but I do all my own material. Each of the bookstore employees are tasked with doing at least two reviews every month. They don't have to be long, just why I loved this book. That way, they can talk about the books to customers too." Deek talked a little about setting up author visits and the things an author shouldn't do. Then he turned back to Tammy. "Anything else?"

"You guys have a writer group that meets at your store, don't you?" When Deek nodded, Tammy turned to Andi and asked her to talk a bit about what the Aspen Hills group was like. And when Andi was done, Tammy was smiling. "See, bookstores are the new gathering place, the new saloon without the drinks. Now, let's talk about the books that are flying off the shelves right now and why, from a bookseller's perspective."

Tammy was really good at this, Cat thought as she tucked the last of the signed books back into the box Tammy had given her. She had fifteen minutes still to shop before Seth would be back to pick her up. After Tammy finished her presentation, the group disbanded and the others joined her in looking through the stacks for the perfect read. Cat took the two books she'd found up to the checkout area. "Your presentation was really informative. You should write an article for one of the writers magazines on it."

"What authors need to know about a bookstore?" Tammy rang up Cat's purchases and then gave her a frequent flyer discount as she called it. "I've actually approached a couple of magazines to see if they'd be interested. Great minds, I guess."

"I hope someone takes you up on it. It's a great topic and one authors have to learn by trial by fire when they're trying to promote." Cat handed her a credit card.

"Fingers crossed," Tammy answered as she ran the credit card. "Oh, you wouldn't believe what happened this week. I was stocking my new arrivals, and this man walked in. I thought I was seeing a ghost. The guy looked exactly like Tom Cook."

"You're kidding," Cat looked around the room, trying to see where Linda was at. "What did you do?"

"You know me, I can't keep my opinions to myself. I told him that he looked like someone, and he laughed and said, Tom Cook, right?" Tammy put the books into a bag and handed Cat back her card. "We talked for a bit. I guess he's always getting that. He told me it had happened more when Tom was alive. Then he bought a book and left."

"What book did he buy?"

Tammy paused for a second. Then as the answer came to her, she grinned, "A book Tom Cook wouldn't ever buy. *The History of Aspen Hills, Colorado*. Tom knew everything about this town."

When Seth came to pick her up, Cat had been standing in the window, watching for him. She needed some time to think. Just because Tom Cook had a doppelganger that looked just like him and was in Aspen Hills, didn't mean that it was Tom's brother. Life was weird that way.

CHAPTER
TWELVE

When Seth took her back to the house, she wondered if she should have gone to the college. Tried to find someone who might have known Tom Cook. Or Jewel for that matter. The answer had to be with Jewel. Cat was more and more certain that Jewel hadn't had an affair with Tom. Maybe she'd been lying, or she'd been lied to, but there just wasn't any evidence of that except for her word. Cat didn't want to blame the victim, but Linda was certain that her husband hadn't cheated. Linda was certain; therefore, Cat was as well.

Cat closed her eyes before she got out of the car.

"What's wrong?" Seth turned off the vehicle and turned to her. "I can hear you thinking way over here."

"What if I'm blaming Jewel because I don't want to look at Linda?" Cat blurted out the one thing she hadn't wanted to say.

"I don't think you're blaming Jewel just because you don't think she had an affair with Tom. And sticking up for your friend is admirable." Seth reached out and tucked a curl under her cap. 'The problem is, no matter who she was or wasn't sleeping with, Jewel's dead. Someone killed her. That's the problem you should be working on, not the Tom angle."

"But that's the thing, it's all tied up. If Tom and Jewel were having an affair, Linda has motive. If not, then Jewel lied and might be lying about things, which could be a motive." Cat shrugged. "I hate to disagree with you, but it's important to know. The problem is I'm running into a dead end and there's the fact that Jewel was pregnant. Did she know? Did she go to a doctor? Did she tell her partner?"

"All good questions. Maybe you should talk to Shirley." Seth pulled the keys out of the car and tucked them into his pocket. "And we both should go inside before I have to restart the car to keep us warm. Shauna will think we're making out in here."

"Which will make her extremely happy. She's been in a mood since you and I broke up." Cat opened the door and climbed out of the van. "What do you think about her plan to get us on a vacation in a week or so?"

Seth rubbed his hands and blew on them before putting an arm around Cat and hurrying her to the front door. "As long as it's tropical, I don't care where we go."

"You're easy to please," Cat hurried into the house and took off her coat and boots. "Let's go have lunch and talk about options."

When the writers got back to the house, Cat met them at the foyer. "I thought we'd talk about your goals this evening and the results of the retreat. The King or Queen Word race winner will be announced tomorrow at dinner, but you have until three pm tomorrow to update the sheet, then it will be taken down."

"I'm getting that cup this retreat," Deek warned the others. He looked at Ryan. "Unless someone's been banking words."

Ryan winked at Cat. "Now why would I do that? Oh, Cat, do you have some time to chat about Tom Cook this afternoon? I'd like to get your thoughts on some research I've been doing."

Cat nodded. "I'd forgotten that you wanted some time. Sorry. Of course. I'm available now if that works."

Ryan headed to the stairs. "Give me ten minutes and I'll meet you in the lobby."

"Does anyone else need some one-on-one time? If so, you better get time scheduled. I'll be in my office most of tomorrow morning if you want to pop by." When no one said anything, she moved to the dining room. "I need coffee."

Linda followed her into the room. "Thanks for putting up with me this week. Ever since that woman accosted me on Saturday night, I've been on edge, waiting for the next shoe to drop. I need you to know that I still don't think Tom was having an affair."

"I thought we'd have more time to chat as well," Cat said. She poured her coffee. "How close were you with Boyd?"

"Tom's brother? Not very close. Tom didn't like to talk about him." She poured coffee, then sweetened it. "I think something happened between them before we married. Whatever it was, it had to be big for Tom to cut someone out of his life like he did. Tom was the most forgiving person I knew."

She pulled a copy of *Alice in Wonderland* out of her backpack. "I picked this up at the bookstore for Tom's niece, Matty. She lives with her mom. Carol divorced Boyd a few years ago after another affair. She calls me occasionally and talks about getting on with her life. A skill I need to learn. I don't think I'm meant to be a widow forever."

"It has to be hard," Cat said.

"You lost your first husband. You must know how it feels." Linda tucked the book away.

Cat shook her head. "Michael and I were divorced several years before he died. I'm not a widow, technically. I did my grieving for the relationship when we divorced. The what could be."

"It's still grieving." Linda met Cat's gaze. "In case you're wondering, I didn't kill Jewel over some angry words. Besides she told Piper that she and Tom had started dating a few years ago. She needed to look Tom up online. He's been dead longer than that."

As Cat made her way to the living room to meet up with Ryan, she wondered what Jewel's game had been. She was obviously in a relationship when she died. She just hadn't been seeing Tom Cook. Or at least not Linda's deceased husband. Unless Tom was a zombie.

She turned to watch Linda go upstairs to her room. Linda had seen someone who looked like Tom. Maybe the zombie theory wasn't that far off. She sat down and opened her notebook. Maybe there was something she'd missed. Maybe Jewel's lover had followed her from New Jersey. She wished she had access to Jewel's manuscript. It could have clues to who this man was that she'd thought of as Tom Cook.

Cat texted her uncle as she waited for Ryan. *Do you have Jewel's laptop? I'd like to read the project she was working on. Maybe it has clues.*

The responding text came back fast. *Shirley's already reading it. I wondered what took you so long to ask. I'll send you a copy.*

Cat should have known that finding Jewel dead would have Shirley involved with the investigation. She decided to find her as soon as this Ryan thing was done. She made herself a note while she waited.

Ryan bustled into the living room. He had a notebook, his phone, and a small tripod. He set everything on the coffee table, then adjusted things on the table. "I'd like to videotape this interview if you don't mind. I'll take notes, but if I forget something, I can go back and look at it."

"That's fine. As long as you don't post the interview on social media. I'm not really camera ready." Cat laughed as she pulled her hair back into a clip again.

"Don't worry about it. Like I told Jewel, it's really just so I can remember what you said. And I'm really glad I did tape her since she's like gone now. People with first-hand information to tell us are dying all the time and we are failing to make sure we have an oral history file. I've been interviewing the people at the nursing home in town for another project. Those guys really have some stories to tell." He set up the video, then checked the view. "Okay, I think we're ready."

"Wait, you interviewed Jewel about her relationship with Tom

Cook? Have you fact checked her information? Her dates?" Cat stared at Ryan's phone. Maybe the information was right there. In Jewel's own words. "Was she worried about something?"

"You mean, did she suspect she was going to die less than twenty-four hours later?" Ryan shook his head. "No, but I haven't transcribed the interview yet. I like to get it down before something happens to a video. Especially since I can't just redo this one, right?"

"Can I watch it?" Cat met Ryan's gaze. "Please?"

"I guess so. Can we finish this interview then I'll let you watch Jewel's. As long as you don't quote her in any publication from this. I don't have her permission to use it for anything but my book." Ryan glanced down at his notes. "She was very specific about that. Especially since I'm using the manuscript for my thesis."

"I promise, I'm not going to use anything in that video in any written work or promotional marketing piece. I just need to hear Jewel's story about her and Tom."

"Tom Cook was a national treasure. He would have won a Pulitzer if he'd lived. His works will be taught in colleges across the world for years in the future. Jewel's story was full of holes. She was just trying to make a buck. Like those women who said they slept with Kennedy after his death." Ryan closed his eyes, breathing through his nose. When he opened them, he watched Cat for a long minute, chewing on the cap of his pen as he did. Then he nodded. "I trust you. As soon as we're done here, I'll show you the video."

Cat could barely concentrate on the questions Ryan was asking. Ryan was clearly one of Tom Cook's biggest fans. But thinking about what she'd known about Tom Cook as a student at Covington as well as a brief attendant of her first writers' retreat, allowed her to focus her mind on who Tom Cook portrayed himself to be.

Every author she knew had a public side and a personal side. The authors she'd met and liked, personally, those two sides were close to being the same person. It was when an author's about page was totally different than their personal life that she had issues with the author. They didn't seem authentic to her and you could tell it in their words. Both written and personal.

When they were done, true to his word, Ryan turned on the video to show Jewel's interview. Cat picked up her pen and wrote down Saturday's date. The interview took place at the Denver airport. Seth must have gone looking for another one of the retreaters when Ryan had started interviewing.

Cat started writing down pieces of Jewel's story. Her uncle would need this information. She was just looking for something to research. Jewel wasn't here anymore to tell her story. She wrote down names, dates, places. Jewel had been very detailed with her information, but like Linda had said with her conversation with Piper, it all happened after Tom had died.

As Ryan finished the interview, Jewel leaned forward, staring into the phone. Chills flowed down Cat's spine as she listened to Jewel's words.

"You're going to think I'm lying until you find out the truth. Then you're going to realize, I was telling you the truth all this time. All I have to do is call one reporter and tell them what I know. I'm just not sure I'm ready to reveal all, so to speak. There's no coming back, once you open Pandora's box, right?"

The screen went black. Cat took a breath, then looked at Ryan. "That's all of it?"

He nodded. "After that last question, Jewel had ended the taping. I realized later that Seth was coming down the corridor from finding Linda Cook from her gate at that exact moment. Weird, huh?"

Cat stood. "Definitely weird. Thanks for letting me watch that."

"No skin off my nose," Ryan stood as well. "I'm probably not even including anything she said in my thesis. I'll see you at the Night Games."

"Yeah, thanks," Cat wandered off and into the kitchen. Shirley and Shauna were sitting at the table. Shirley was reading something on her phone, and Shauna was paging through a cookbook.

"What's going on?" Cat got a bottle of water out of the fridge and sat down at the table with the two women.

"She's reading and I'm researching new menus," Shauna said, not looking up as she focused on a recipe. "Dinner isn't until five. Are you hungry now?"

"No, just thinking about Jewel." Cat turned to Shirley. "Uncle Pete says you're reading her manuscript. Any news?"

"She was never going to sell this thing." Shirley handed Cat the phone. "Read this page. I feel like I'm drowning in a pit of anger and self-pity."

Cat read the section and handed Shirley back her phone. "She sounds crazy."

"I can't confirm that from a medical diagnosis, but I agree with your statement. Jewel wrote about ten pages ago that she was a direct descendant of Napoleon and Josephine. And that she had a million-dollar contract to sell this book." Shirley set the phone down. "If the evidence didn't point to her being murdered, I'd say she had staged this whole thing and thought someone would find her before she died."

Shauna looked up. "I hadn't thought about that angle."

"I don't think you can stab yourself with a fireplace poker." Cat shook her head. "If anything, it proves that she had help with this whole book idea. And that she wasn't able to pull it off on her own. I'm glad you're here though. I want to run an idea past you."

Night games started promptly at seven on Friday night. All of the writers, Shauna, and Cat were milling around the room when Deek asked everyone to find a seat. "We've got a bit of a change in process for tonight's session. Since we'll be eating together tomorrow night, we'll have one last writing session together here at ten. And don't miss setting your wake-up alarm Sunday morning. Seth says we need to leave here at nine to make everyone's connections at the airport."

Cat watched as several people took notes or set an alarm on their phone.

Shauna raised her hand. "Friendly reminder that breakfast will be served on Sunday morning, but it will be set out at seven, so if you want to eat before you leave, add in that time too."

"It's going to take me a week to get back into my normal routine when I get home," Piper responded. "No breakfast waiting for me. I'll have to cook my own food. And, I need to start the diet that was on my new year's resolutions. I'll miss this place."

"It's like a magical house for writers," Andi nodded. "I live in town and I'm still going to go through withdrawal symptoms. I'm still petitioning for Cat and Seth to adopt me so I can live here forever."

"Now, Andi, you know they can't adopt everyone who comes through the retreat." Deek winked at Cat. "And besides, I'm first on the list. My mom has even signed over all parental responsibilities to make it happen."

Cat laughed as she stood to take over the podium from Deek. "Well, Deek's right about us not having the room to adopt all of you, but Shauna set up a Facebook page for all of our reunion writers. You'll be added to the group Sunday before you get on your flight, or arrive home," she smiled at Andi and Ryan. "Make sure you keep in touch. We want to help you celebrate your wins even when you're not here."

She looked around the room at the retreaters. "You'll also be getting a survey that asks how your week at the retreat went. We want the good and the bad. And, please think about the effect the reunion guests, Andi, Deek, Linda, and Shirley had on your week. I want to know how this change affects everyone. Would it be better to do two different retreats? Was having the reunion guests helpful or distracting? And if there isn't room or you think a question should be added to the survey, email me or Shauna. Even if you mention it to one of us in the next few days, getting it in writing will remind us. So let's start with your goal setting plans. Who wants to go first?"

Linda held up her hand. "I'd like to share, if I can."

"Of course," Cat looked around the room. "Then Linda can pick the next person to go."

"I'll be picked last. Just like in gym class," Felix mumbled. Then he shook his head. "Just kidding. I rocked at dodge ball."

Linda carried up a sheet of paper. "I knew this was coming so I wrote down some notes. You all know I lost my husband a few years ago. Since that time, I've been trying to find out who Linda Cook is besides being the wife of Tom Cook, the author. Or now, Tom's widow. I've been holding on to things that he loved, just because I thought I should. Like the cabin here in Aspen Hills. Well, I've decided that this year is going to be the year of Linda Cook. I'm going to do everything I had put aside to support Tom. First off, I'm finishing my memoir and then I'm going to write a woman's fiction novel. One for me."

"That's awesome, Linda." Andi glanced at Cat. "My mom is kind of going through the same things. She said she's always been someone's daughter or wife or mother. Now she wants to know who she is just by herself."

Linda wiped her cheeks. "Exactly. So that's my goal planning. I have a lot more details and techniques on my sheet, but mostly it's about finding who I am on my own. And visiting England. I've always wanted to go."

She started to move from the lectern but then realized she was supposed to pick the next person. "Okay, Felix, come on up and tell us all about your plans to be a professional dodge ball player."

The group chuckled as they changed places. Linda sat next to Cat. "That was awesome. I love your plan."

She patted Cat's arm. "It takes a village to raise a child and mourn a lost love. I appreciate you and Shauna always being there for me. If you have a woman's fiction group coming up, let me know and I'll come and pick their brains on the manuscript."

By the time they got through the goal planning, it was already eight. Shauna called for a break. "The dining room is filled with more treats so go get your sugar high on. We'll meet back here for a retreat recap at eight fifteen."

Cat stood. "Change of plans. We'll do the retreat recap Sunday morning before you leave for the airport. Deek will be running word sprints when we come back. I don't know about you, but I need some words on the paper."

"Butt in chair time," Piper responded. "I'm going to miss these sessions."

THIRTEEN

S hirley caught up with Cat in the foyer before she went to get some coffee for the writing sprint. "I'm heading back to Pete's house. He just texted me and said he was home."

"Then I'll see you tomorrow?" Cat gave Shirley a hug.

"Not until dinner, unless Pete gets a break in the case and leaves me alone." She walked over to get her coat. "I'd extend my visit, but if the case is still going on, it kind of defeats the purpose."

"We're always glad to see you so if you want to come over while Uncle Pete's working, you're more than welcome. Even if there isn't a formal retreat going on." Cat watched as a cab pulled up to the doorway. "I take it that's for you?"

"Yep, Pete said he called one for me. He doesn't like me walking at night alone. Of course, at home in Alaska, it's too cold to walk much at night anyway." Shirley paused as she started to leave. "For what it's worth, I agree with you. I don't think Linda killed Jewel. She's way too open with her feelings to be able to hide something like that."

Cat considered Shirley's thoughts as she got ready for the word sprints. She needed coffee or cocoa along with at least one of Shauna's chocolate chip cookies. She headed to the dining room and was surprised to find Seth there, chatting with Wilder. When she came inside, he waved her over to where they sat.

"Wilder said he's going to send me his goal setting habit's template and use me as a guinea pig. What do you think?" Seth slapped Wilder on the back. "I might just get on a routine like all of you writer folks."

"A lot of writers don't have a routine," Wilder clarified. "I think Seth's the perfect person to try out my system on an non-academic. He's going to have many different goals and to do lists than a writer or a student would have. This way, I can prove to any publisher who takes on the book that it's not just for word people like us."

"I think that's a perfect plan," Cat responded. "I've read way too many books on goal setting that only focused on one part of our lives. Work or home or even the spiritual side. We need something that has room for more than just meetings and word goals set and hit."

Seth stared at her. "You get it."

"I always have," she answered. "I need some coffee if I have a chance at making this brain work for twenty-five minutes, if not longer."

Cat could feel Seth's gaze on her back as she walked away. She wondered why he hadn't known that she understood who he was before this. But better late than just living on assumptions about each other. She grabbed her cookies and decided to go with the hot cocoa when an alarm on Deek's watch went off.

"Time to go make the donuts," he called as he headed out into the hallway, grabbing a handful of cookies on the way out.

Seth waved at her as she followed the group out of the dining room. "No rest for the wicked, right? I'll clear this mess and load up the dishwasher. You and Shauna go play with your friends."

～

THE NEXT MORNING, as Cat got ready for the day, a thought occurred to her. As soon as she was dressed, she hurried to her office, without coffee. She looked through the files Shauna had made on each participant, finally opening Ryan's. She found the name of his referring professor who was also his thesis advisor. She composed a quick email and hoped the professor was one of those who checked their emails on weekends.

Then she headed downstairs for coffee. Shauna was in the kitchen, just pulling out a batch of cinnamon rolls. "Good morning, how late did you stay up writing?"

Cat grabbed a cup and filled it with coffee. "Too late. I did two more sprints after you left. And Deek and the guys were still going strong when I called it a night. It's like no one wanted to say uncle first."

"Winter retreats are much more productive since the gang doesn't hang out at the bar at night." Shauna cut out a roll and set it in front of Cat. "Shirley left early."

"She wanted some time with Uncle Pete." Cat broke off a piece of the roll. "So good. Anyway, I figure I'll see if anyone wants a last get together this afternoon. At least with me. Anything you need from me?"

Shauna got a cinnamon roll for herself, then sat down. "Remember that Pete and Shirley are coming to dinner on Sunday night. And we have a house meeting on Monday morning to pick our tropical beach destination plan. I've got three choices for you guys to choose from."

"Do we have dates?" Cat glanced at the calendar.

"Not yet, but I'm thinking the second week of February. We'll drop the retreat guests off on Sunday and leave the next Wednesday. Sunshine here we come." Shauna glanced at her to do list. "Andi said she'd come over and stay at the house while we're gone to feed Snow and the dwarves. I asked her to stay so people didn't think the house was empty. The frats have been playing a few practical jokes this winter. Oh, and Mrs. Rice will be home on Sunday. I'm making her dinner that night but I'd like to invite her over here on Wednesday night for dinner."

"Do you want me here?" Cat sipped her coffee.

"That's kind of the point. To get everyone together." Shauna set her fork down. "You can be nice for one dinner."

"Yes, of course. I'm probably just tired right now. I'll put it on my calendar." Inside, Cat groaned. The week after a retreat it took her days to recover from all the in person chatting. Now she had not one but two new social events that would just delay her recharging from running the retreat. "And I'll be attending one last counselling session on Monday."

Shauna looked at her calendar. "Seth told me you guys were done with therapy. I took it off the house schedule."

Cat stood and took her empty plate to the sink. Then she grabbed the carafe Shauna had filled and had waiting for her. "We are. I just get to deliver the news in person to our shrink. I don't think she'll be happy. But I will."

Cat worked until nine when she went downstairs to talk to the writers. Everyone was in the dining room, eating and talking about their projects. Cat stood in the doorway, watching them chat. This was exactly how she'd seen the house when she'd bought it with Michael. Filled with writers talking about their writing and books and classes. The house was happy, even if it hadn't been fulfilled exactly in the way she and Micheal had envisioned the idea. He'd wanted to rent out rooms to students. Kind of a sorority or fraternity house that students from far away could call home.

Cat's writers' retreat was a different type of home for writers trying to find themselves. Find their voice. And learn that being true to yourself was the first step in writing a great book.

"Hey Cat, are you eating with us?" Felix stood next to her. He'd gotten up from his conversation with Piper and Wilder on goal setting and their different approaches. "I needed another cinnamon roll. They are so good."

"Actually, I ate one this morning before I went to my office." Cat came farther into the room. "Writers, I was wondering if you wanted another chat with an author session. Any burning questions that you need to ask? Or do we want to talk about editing processes? Or anything else?"

Felix held up his hand. "I'd love to talk about what happens when you're done with a manuscript. I know we talked a little about the process, but I'm wondering about the timeline. And when to give up on a project."

Cat glanced around the room. "So the timeline of becoming a published author is on the table. Any other subjects?"

"What do you do all day? Right now, I'm writing in between everything. My work, my life. What happens if I'm lucky enough to be a full-time author? How does my life look when that happens?" Piper asked.

Linda held up her hand. "I'm lucky to be there, but I have no idea how to schedule my day as an author. That would really be helpful."

"Okay," Cat answered. "There's two process or timeline questions. What else?"

"Can we ask them in the session," Deek asked. He held up a finger. "I know. I don't know what I don't know, so what should I know?"

Cat laughed. "I'm not sure I caught all those twists, but yeah, we can talk about that too."

"Then ten this morning? We're going to the Diner for lunch one last time." Deek glanced around the table.

"Like I need any more food. I think I could not eat for days and be fine." Piper laughed as she broke off another bite of cinnamon roll.

"I'll see you all in an hour, then." Cat turned away and headed to the kitchen to see what Shauna was doing. Seth was in the kitchen alone. "Oh, hey. I figured you were resting today since you get to play designated driver for dinner tonight."

"I'm fine. Sam's a little antsy so I'm going to take him out to play ball for a bit. I was just refilling my coffee so I don't freeze out there."

Seth held up his cup. "What about you? Writing or writers this morning?"

"A little of both. I was writing before, but now I'm doing a session at ten." She went over to fill a travel mug. "I drank all my coffee upstairs. I think I can have one more cup before I get the jitters."

"You're a light weight." He kissed her on the forehead. "I'll run into you later. Looking forward to dinner tonight."

Cat followed him out as soon as her cup was filled, but he'd already gone back to his apartment in the west wing. She headed back upstairs to write a little more. Or clean out her email. That always took a few minutes and would burn time while she waited. Sometimes, her head was too fuzzy to actually write, so she made up ideas to do something, anything besides writing. When she opened her email, she found she had a response from Ryan's thesis advisor. She opened the email and read it.

According to Professor Henry, Ryan had changed his thesis away from heroes from Aspen Hills. The professor had warned him that it was too narrow. That Covington graduates that had gone on to be successful as writers were few and far between. Unless you counted those who wrote genre fiction. Many Covington graduate students could only get jobs in academia, and more likely, only at Covington. Cat pushed away the implied insult that since she wrote popular fiction, she wasn't a real writer. This professor didn't think that Tom Cook had been a real writer. The email ended with a paragraph about how Ryan was now working on examining the works of Ernest Hemingway, in particular, the works penned while he lived in Paris.

Cat sat back and frowned. That wasn't what Ryan was working on. Had he lied to his professor or to her? Many times, students sent to the retreat had told her that they were writing something that they couldn't tell their Covington advisors. Mostly because the work wasn't literary enough. Was this just Ryan's way of writing something he wanted to write without the college finding out?

Or was this something completely different?

Either way, she didn't have any more time right now to ponder this twist. She needed to be downstairs in less than ten minutes. And she hadn't pulled her notes from the last additional session lecture she'd sketched out.

She grabbed her file and a notebook and headed back downstairs. As Seth always said, it was time to play with her writer friends. Of course, he also called her writing time playing with her imaginary friends. It was all play. Which Cat agreed with and that was why being an author was the best job in the world. At least when the play was going well.

All the writers were gathered in the living room waiting when she got downstairs. Well, all but Shirley, and Ryan. She knew where Shirley was, but she turned to Deek. He'd probably know. "Do we know if Ryan will be joining us?"

Deek shook his head. "He had a meeting with his thesis advisor. He wanted to try to get him to change his mind and let him write on a different subject."

Cat hoped that the professor wouldn't tell Ryan that she'd been asking about his project. If the subject came up, she'd tell him that she'd just wanted to help mold his week. And that the email must have gotten lost. Of course, she'd totally be caught in the lie if the professor had printed out or showed the date on the email to Ryan. Maybe she needed a different excuse. Something about ending the retreat by planning for the future and learning how to get your projects completed? It sounded as good as any excuse if he asked.

"Shirley's not here either," Piper called out.

Cat pulled her chair closer to the group. "She's on a date with my uncle. They're an item if she hadn't told you before. So if he has free time, she's going to spend it with him this week. She'll be at dinner with us though."

Linda opened her notebook. "Is it too late to start all over on a new project? I'm sure I won't be named Word Queen, but I have a few ideas I'd like to bounce off you guys at the end of Cat's session. I'm looking for what excites you guys the most."

"Like Nashville hot chicken wings?" Felix frowned and rubbed his stomach. "I guess I'm hungry."

Cat wrote the words, Linda's brainstorming, on the flipchart. Then she added the life cycle of a book. She turned back to the group. "Anything else?"

Piper raised her hand again, "When to give up on a project. I've queried this project for months and I've gotten a few requests for full reads but no actual bites from an agent. And with non-fiction, you have to have that agent in place."

"Unless you want to self-publish," Wilder suggested. "You may not make as much money and you'll have to put out some cash to get it ready. A cover, an editor, maybe some tools for you to use, like something to format the book with. But then you get all of the money without an agent and a publisher getting a portion."

"And all the hassles," Felix added as the group laughed.

Cat wrote on the whiteboard – Traditional versus Self-publishing and When to give up hope. "Okay that's probably all we'll get to this session, but we might have more time at the end to fill with a few more questions. Let's talk about these in this order, writing process or how; timeframe for traditional and a timeline for self-publishing, and then the final discussion will be on when to give up. Then we'll give the floor to Linda and you can help her hone her new project ideas. Sound good?" She wrote numbers 1 to 4 on the page next to each item. No one's hand went up as she scanned the room. "Okay, then let's get busy."

Cat sat down and held out a calendar. "I appreciated Professor Presley's presentation this session because it focused on a system. Now, I'm not saying you have to use his system to be a successful author, but you do have to have a system. Piper, Felix, and Wilder, all three of you have developed a system that not only works for you, but you think might work for others, which is why you're writing a book about it."

The three nodded as Cat spoke. "But the one thing you need to make sure is you have room in your universe for other systems, for other thoughts. I don't care if you write five hundred words a day, or five thousand. I don't care if you write weekdays or every day of the week until you hit a word count goal. You can write with pen and paper or in a Word document or in Scrivener. But it has to be a system and a tool that works for you."

"I read that if you don't write every day, you're not a writer," Piper added.

"Does a plumber fix a sink every day?" Cat asked with a smile. "When I'm writing a book or drafting the first version, I try to write as many days in a row that I can. It keeps me in the story. But if I'm in Denver all day, I'm not going to let it kill my progress. And sometimes, you need head space to think out a plot problem."

"So you're saying there's no system." Wilder looked confused.

Cat shook her head. "No, I'm saying you need to find a system that works for you. I can tell you my system, my goals, but they may not work with your lifestyle. If I didn't have help for the retreat, I probably wouldn't be writing this week. There would be too many other problems to deal with."

Deek wagged his finger at her. "It's not nice to call us problems to our face. That's something you write in your diary so we can find out later we were pains in your buttocks."

"That's not what I meant," Cat smiled anyway. "All I'm trying to say is it might take you a while before you find a system that works. And you might have to change it if your life changes. Or if challenges come up."

"Like someone dying during a retreat," Ryan asked as he came into the room. "Like Tom Cook did on your first retreat and now, Jewel has continued the tradition of a retreat participant dying on your watch."

CHAPTER

FOURTEEN

"Dude, that wasn't nice to say," Deek stood up as Ryan came into the room. "It's not Cat's fault that people die. My little tourist town seems to have more murders per capita than Los Angeles down the road, but we don't blame the mayor or the bookstore owner."

"It's true though," Wilder pulled a chair into the circle for Ryan to sit down. "The retreat has a bit of a reputation of being Murder Central."

"My professor said the college tried to cancel their sponsorship, but Cat has friends in high places. Isn't that right?" Ryan sat down and crossed his arms, staring at her.

"Dude..." Deek started but Cat held up her hand, motioning Deek to sit down.

"Nice to have you join us, Ryan. Yes, Tom Cook died here, but no one visiting the retreat or the three of us who staff the retreat killed him. The college sponsors the retreat because we let a student, like you, come for free. The sponsorship isn't financial, it's allowing us to use the library for the week we have guests here. And we pay a fee for that now. It's a win, win for both of us." She looked around the room.

"We had one incident where a retreater was responsible for a death, but we put in safeguards after that, including the fact that the local police department runs background checks on all of you before you get here to try to screen for violent behavior."

"Ryan, I think you owe Cat an apology. You've been weird since Jewel died. Did you know her?" Piper leaned forward, watching Ryan for clues.

"No, I mean, I've heard of someone claiming to be Cook's mistress, but I thought it was all baloney. And when I interviewed her, the dates were all off. She said she met him after the day of his death." Ryan looked at Cat. "Look, I'm sorry I came in all upset. My professor said you were just trying to profit off of Tom Cook's death. Bring people in to see where he died. He said you were trying to get me to change my thesis."

"But you knew that wasn't true," Cat added.

Ryan nodded. "He assumed you were behind the visit since you emailed him to see what I was studying. He'd thought I'd moved on to the subject he told me to write."

Cat let out a breath. "So are we good? I did email him to see if there was anything I could help you with after the session. And honestly, I wanted to know if you were obsessed with Tom Cook."

"To see if I killed Jewel." Ryan nodded. "That makes sense, but I didn't kill Jewel. I was on the snowshoe adventure, then I was with Deek the rest of the day. We were playing cards here at the school until late that night."

"He's telling the truth," Deek confirmed Ryan's story.

"Okay, so we have that off our chest," Cat looked at her white-board. "Let's get back to the session topics we decided on. Next up, how long does it take to be published by a traditional house."

Cat left the group when they started brainstorming with Linda on a new story idea. She sank into the chair outside the room and closed her eyes. Professors at Covington would never understand why she would have left academia to write popular fiction and run a writers' retreat. How could she want this more than tenure?

"You look like you need a friend," Seth sat next to her and wrapped his arm around her shoulder, pulling her close. "Bad session?"

"The college is never going to forgive me for leaving teaching and going to write full time. I'm suspicious in their minds because I'm doing what I love. And people dying around me is the work of the devil as well." She laughed as she leaned her head on his shoulder. "Me, I'm the devil."

"You are not. You're a bit controlling and you have a horrible temper, especially when you're mad at me. But you're caring and worry about your friends and for some reason that I never could understand, you love me." He wiped tears off her cheeks. "It's last day jitters. Everyone will be gone tomorrow afternoon and you can go soak in a tub or stalk your uncle until he lets you help with finding Jewel's killer. You don't give up this easily. What's wrong that you're not telling me?"

Cat leaned back onto the bench. There was something nagging at her and making her senses tingle. She'd thought it was Ryan, but now that he'd confronted her as the possible killer, she didn't think he'd killed Jewel. He was looking for whom ever had killed one of their own, just like the rest of them. "Honestly, I feel like I'm missing something. Every time we bring up the subject of who killed Jewel, I come up with a different angle, and yet, I still feel like I'm missing something important."

"Let's go to the kitchen. Your writers will be leaving for lunch soon and you don't want them to see that even successful professional authors can have bad days." Seth stood and pulled her up to join him. "Besides, you always feel better after you eat."

In the kitchen, they found Shirley at the table, talking to Shauna who was stirring what smelled like potato sausage soup. Shauna turned to them and frowned. "What's wrong?"

"Cat's having a personal crisis because she can't figure out who killed Jewel." Seth led her to a chair. "That soup smells amazing. Is it ready?"

"Almost. We're waiting for the rolls. Get her a soda. She'll perk up with some sugar in her." Shauna nodded to the fridge.

"You guys are talking about me like I'm not here." Cat grumbled as she met Shirley's concerned gaze. "Oh, please, not you too."

"One, I need to remind you that you aren't supposed to be investigating a murder in Aspen Hills. That's what they pay your uncle for." Shirley picked up her phone and handed it to Cat. "And two, we have a phone number of one of Jewel's contacts. It's a burner phone that was bought in Connecticut."

"Connecticut, like where Tom Cook's brother lives?" Cat looked at the number and then wrote it down on the back of an envelope.

"Maybe. So far, no one's answered when Pete calls. I came over here to try a different phone. My cell has an Alaskan area code. It screams scam call. But if a call came from Aspen Hills and not the police station or local city numbers, maybe someone would pick up." Shirley glanced at the other three. "Who wants to try?"

Shauna took the envelope from Cat. "Let me. I can say that she gave this number as an emergency contact."

"Give it a go," Seth nodded.

Shauna sat down and put the call on speaker. Then she dialed. When a man answered, she introduced herself. "Good afternoon, this is Shauna Clodagh from Warm Springs Writers' Retreat in Aspen Hills. This number was listed as an emergency contact for Jewel Doan. Who am I speaking with?"

"Jewel Doan, I'm afraid I don't know that name," a man replied.

"That's strange. The phone she left in our care has this number called several times for long conversations. Does someone else have access to your phone?" Shauna tried to sound confused.

"That must be it. I'm a high school teacher and debate coach. Sometimes my kids use the phone when I'm out of my classroom. Probably one of the kids."

"Oh, my. That's unfortunate. Do you think Jewel might have been a parent to one of your students? Has anyone said their mom is out of town? We're still trying to reach Jewel's next of kin." Shauna met Cat's gaze as she talked.

Cat had to admit, Shauna was great at making up a story on the fly. But she still hadn't gotten the man's name.

"No, and I'm sorry, I've got to go. I'm driving and I just passed a cop. I don't want to be pulled over for talking on my phone." The line went dead.

"So a teacher and a debate coach at a high school. That sounds like Tom's brother, doesn't it?" Cat looked around the room. "Was Jewel having an affair with the wrong brother?"

WHEN THE GROUP got to the restaurant, everyone was ready to celebrate their accomplishments that week. As the writers munched on nachos and drank strawberry margaritas, Cat pulled out her list of accomplishments. She listed off the number of words both for the group and on an average per person. "We expected the total number of words to increase with this group because of more people, but unexpectedly, the average number of words per person increased as well. So did having the reunion guests challenge the rest of you? Or are you all just abnormally focused on goal achievement?"

"Well, since three of us are writing goal setting books, I'd blame the latter explanation. But I think there was some advantage to having the old guys here," Piper snuck a glance at Deek.

"Hey!" Deek said through a mouth full of nachos.

As the group laughed, Felix continued the discussion. "Actually, I think Piper's right. Not about Deek being old but having someone who went through the sessions before gave me, at least, a better idea of what was going to happen this week. And what my role in being an active participant meant."

"Yeah, I felt like I was responsible for making the week work for me." Wilder added to the discussion. He dished out more nachos onto his plate. "I went over my goal sheet I wrote at the beginning of the week, and I'd exceeded all my expectations. I don't know if it was because of the Night Games or just the group expectation that I'd be working on my project."

"I got to talk to a lot of people in the area who knew Tom Cook," Ryan shyly smiled at Linda. "I know my professors aren't keen on this project, and maybe I'll need to change it up later, but I want to finish this manuscript. Then I can decide to shelve it or not."

Cat liked the fact that Ryan was committed to his project. His professors weren't as convinced that his theory was appropriate, but she wondered if it was just a fear of shining a light on the alumni of Covington. When most of your student body base were related to a mob family, having scholarship students, like Ryan, look into the history of the school's graduates was problematic. "Well, Ryan, you're in luck because even if the college isn't supporting your old thesis, you're local so you can use me as an unofficial mentor on the project."

Shauna and Seth stared at her. She gently shook her head, not the time to bring up the problems that Ryan's digging could cause, but if the kid was determined, she wanted to keep an eye on what he was reading and learning so if something did cross a line, she could let Dante know that Ryan wasn't trying to out the school's mob family legacy.

Cat knew she might have to out the school's directives to Ryan but there was a good chance that he'd never find out what the connections were. And if he didn't, an autobiography of Tom Cook probably wouldn't even get a publisher's interest.

"I'd like that," Ryan glanced over at Andi. "I'm joining the writers group at the bookstore too."

"Everyone should find a writers group to join," Deek added. "Writing is such a solitary endeavor. We sit in front of our computer and make up lives for other people. We need to make sure we have lives too."

"Well said," Linda added. "As the wife of a successful author, I know how hard it was for Tom to walk away from a manuscript. Even for a date night."

"My last girlfriend broke up with me because she said I didn't have room in my life for her," Wilder admitted. "I'm going to have to talk to you about ways to keep a relationship going as well as carve out time for writing and a job."

"Well, I'm an expert," Linda glanced around the table. "Tom and I had a lovely marriage. We traveled together. He always made me feel like there was room in his brain for me, even when he was deep into a book and writing stories for his characters. Life is short, make sure you enjoy it. And on that note, I need to visit the little girls room before our meal comes."

As Linda left the table, Ryan glanced at Piper. "I didn't upset her, did I?"

Piper squeezed his arm. "I think she likes talking about Tom. It keeps him in her mind. But let's change the subject before she gets back."

"Sometimes I can be a little direct," Ryan shook his head. "Maybe I'm just not made for social interactions."

"I think you're doing fine," Cat glanced back at her notes. "As soon as Linda gets back, I'll announce the King or Queen of Words. Remember, it comes with an exclusive Warm Springs Retreat mug to remember your accomplishment this week."

"Are reunion guests in the running?" Andi asked. "I've gotten a lot done this week. It's been amazing."

"Of course, you are." Cat said, but then Wilder raised his hand. "Yes?"

"That doesn't seem fair. They knew what was expected when they arrived. You should have two winners. One for the new guys, and gals," he winked at Piper before he continued, "and one for the old guys."

This time, at the description of the reunion guests, Andi threw a tortilla chip at Wilder. Apparently, this 'old guy' joke had been floating around all week. When Linda returned, Cat stood. "Okay, the King or Queen of Words for this session, is…"

She paused before announcing the winner, looking around the table. She froze when she saw Linda's face. She looked shocked. "Linda, what's wrong?"

Linda took a long sip of her margarita. "I think I must be tired or something. Maybe it's being here or maybe I should visit my doctor when I get home."

"Linda, tell us what's wrong." Piper turned toward her.

"You know how I thought I saw Tom in town a few days ago? It just happened again." Linda nodded toward the bar area. "When I came out of the bathroom, he was standing there at the pick-up line, waiting for food."

Seth stood, but Cat waved him back down. "Did he see you?"

Linda shook her head. "I ran to the table."

Cat wondered if this was just a coincidence. She needed to keep this from the writers though. No use getting everyone, especially Ryan and Linda, worked up. "Hey Seth, would you go to the bar and get me a beer? The margaritas seem sweet today."

"Sure," he stood, but when he passed by her, she grabbed his arm. "Watch to see if anyone answers Shauna's call."

Seth met Shauna's gaze and nodded. She gave him time to reach the area, then pulled out her phone. She stood and excused herself from the group. "Sorry, I forgot to call the vet about Snow. She has a bit of a limp."

After they left the table, Cat texted her uncle.

"What about the word winner?" Felix asked as she finished her text.

"Oh, let's wait for Seth and Shauna to get back. They want to be part of the celebration." Cat nodded toward the waitress who was carrying a tray toward the table. "And our food's here."

"First we're waiting for Linda, now Seth and Shauna," Piper shook her head. "Good thing the food's here to distract us. Cat you really know how to build up the tension. I guess it's all the fiction writing."

When Shauna came back, she stopped next to Cat. "It's the same guy. Did you call Pete?"

"I texted him that he was needed here. He's not happy, but he sent a car and he'll be here soon." She glanced back to the bar area. "Where's Seth?"

"He's watching the guy. I asked the waitress to stall his order until Pete gets here." Shauna sat down at her plate. Louder, so the writers could hear, "I'm starving. I hope Seth doesn't mind us starting without him, but the line at the bar is long."

"You could probably wave down a waitress," Andi suggested.

Cat stood. "That's a great idea. I'll grab our waitress and then get Seth. Go ahead and eat. I'll be right back."

"Are you sure you don't need help?" Deek asked. The look on his face told her that he knew something was going on besides getting a drink, but she shook her head.

"Eat. Enjoy your meal before it gets cold." Cat hurried away from the table before anyone could ask her another question. Their waitress was coming out of the kitchen as she passed by. "Hey, could you bring a draft beer to my place at the table?"

"Colorado Pilsner?" The woman had been their waitress before and knew what Cat drank.

"Sure, that's fine. I'll be right back." Cat hurried into the bar and found Seth, leaning against a wall, a bottle of beer in his hand. "You're drinking my beer."

"I'm pretending to drink your beer. I'm the designated driver, remember." He handed her the bottle. "He's over there looking at his phone. In the blue jacket by the neon beer sign."

Cat blinked. "He looks just like Tom. That has to be his brother, right?"

"Or a weird doppelganger. They say that there are people who look just alike in the world." Seth turned to her so he wasn't watching the guy anymore, but she could still see him over his shoulder. "We need to look less conspicuous. I don't think he'd like being stared at by me while we wait for your uncle."

Cat saw the uniformed officer walk into the bar right after Seth mention her uncle. He scanned the room from the entrance, then saw her. She could see the question in his eyes. She nodded toward the man in the blue jacket, then saw the officer nod.

As she watched, the officer walked over to the takeout counter and grinned at the woman standing there. "Janice, can you get me a to go order really quick? Taco plate? No beans, just rice."

"Of course, Carl, I'll get that set up for you right now." Janice took off for the kitchen to fill the officer's order. The bar was busy, but not that loud so Cat could hear their conversation. Most of the people there were eating.

"Hey guys, there you are," Deek walked in from the dining room. He glanced at the beer in Cat's hand. "The waitress just delivered your beer. I thought you'd want to know."

Cat smiled and handed Seth the other beer. "I better get back to my writers. Are you going to wait for our guest?"

Deek scanned the bar area, then took Cat's arm as they walked back to the dining room. "That guy really does look like Tom Cook. I take it Seth's waiting for your uncle to show up?"

"You've been here too many times," Cat grinned at Deek.

He shook his head. "I see it all the time at home too. My boss is like you. Always in the wrong place at the right time."

CHAPTER

FIFTEEN

By the time Seth returned to the table, Cat had announced the winner of the word count contest. It was Piper. She'd beat Deek, the next in line by just over a hundred words. "Deek, I'll get you a mug too since Wilder pointed out a flaw in our original plan. Although, I think he thought the reunion guests would come out on top."

"If I wouldn't have been starting a new project, I would have won, easily." Deek explained.

"Sure dude, keep telling yourself that," Piper grinned. "Just remember, you lost to a newbie."

"You're writing non-fiction. You don't have to do world building," Deek grumbled as the group at the table laughed.

As they started to move the party back to the house, Cat paused at the table to pay for the meal. Uncle Pete came up to her. "Hey, any news?"

"I'm going to go have a chat with Boyd Cook at the station now. He has what looks like a really old copy of *Alice in Wonderland* in his tote. It's wrapped in a cloth. Any news on that? He swears he bought it at the bookstore, but I haven't been able to call Tammy to verify his story."

"There's a missing *Alice in Wonderland* from Tom Cook's cabin. Linda had it on a list that she'd asked me to grab from the cabin when I went up with Seth." Cat took her credit card back from the waitress and signed the receipt with a large tip. She tucked her card away in her wallet and stood to walk with her uncle. "I bet Linda could verify if it was the one she was looking for."

"I'll send Shirley over to the house with it this evening. Is everyone leaving tomorrow?"

"Back to reality, yes. I think Seth's taking them at nine." She glanced at the police car that had just left the lot. "Do you think he killed Jewel?"

"Yes, but now I have to prove it. Her journal we got from her room says that Tom was in hiding. That he'd faked his death and then had fallen in love with her. Either the woman was delusional, or she'd been fed a pack of lies. Maybe he hadn't expected her to be here in Aspen Hills or to run into Linda. But whatever, I think we have enough to charge him with stealing the book. And knowing what these things can cost, it might be enough to keep him around for a while. I just hope we have enough to bring justice to that poor woman."

"You'll figure it out. He had her number in his phone. That's a connection at least."

He nodded. "I just hope that he didn't kill her because of the pregnancy. That would just be sad. A new life is ready to come into the world and gets its mom killed in the process."

Cat nodded to the van where she could see several faces staring at her and her uncle. "I better go. I'll tell Linda to expect Shirley's visit."

He put his hat on as he walked toward his car. He paused as he opened the door. "Thanks for the assist with catching this guy. I hate it when you get involved, but I'm thankful for the intel."

"Was that so hard to say?" Cat called back, smiling. She waved and climbed into the SUV. The music was playing lightly, but no one was talking.

Finally, Deek asked, "So what was all of that about?"

"We'll chat when we get back to the house. I need to see if anyone has anything to add to the story anyway." Cat snuggled into the seat and put on her seatbelt. She held her hands against the heater vents. "Boy, it's cold outside."

When they arrived home, the writers gathered in the living room. Cat had pulled Linda aside and told her what her uncle had asked about the book.

"You found it? I'm so happy. But Boyd? He couldn't hurt a fly. His ex-wife, Carol, well, she's going to be furious if this affair is true. She told me just last week they were trying again and she was hopeful. He married money and she keeps a tight hold on the purse strings." Linda shook her head. "I just talked to her yesterday and told her about the books I was sending Matty, her daughter. Boyd's supposed to be in Wisconsin for a teacher conference."

"Where is home?" Cat wondered if Linda's sister-in-law could have been here when Jewel was killed.

"Connecticut. She's a lawyer and I called her at her office. She's been in a trial all week, so we weren't able to connect until Friday. I talked to Matty Thursday night and she complained about how grumpy her mom had been all week at dinner. Well, for almost two weeks. I guess with Boyd gone, they'd been ordering in dinner so Carol didn't have to cook after work." Linda smiled. "Matty said she wanted to learn to cook so she didn't have to eat takeout when her mom was busy. I told her I understood since I got takeout a lot after her uncle died."

Boyd was looking more and more guilty. Shirley came in the front door with a package. They went into the den to look at the book. Shirley gently unwrapped the book and Linda gasped when she saw the cover. "That's Tom's copy. I'm sure of it. Check the front cover. It should be engraved to a little girl named Alice from her grandfather for her birthday. It's a first edition. Tom said the note might have made the value of the book less, but it made a better story in his mind."

Shirley opened the book and they all stared at the engraving. Shirley read aloud the inscription. "Another Alice to enjoy the story. I think Boyd Cook is in trouble."

"What's he saying?" Cat wondered if Shirley would tell them.

Shirley rewrapped the book. "According to our friend, he's just here on a vacation to honor his brother. He says he didn't know Jewel and he didn't know how her number got in his phone. So basically, he's denying everything. But now we have him in the cabin. I bet some of the fingerprints they found and couldn't identify will match Boyd's."

"Can they do a DNA test on the baby?" Cat wondered as Shirley started to leave. Her uncle hadn't been very hopeful."

"Already in process. I'm not sure what they can do, but you know your uncle isn't going to give up until he finds justice for that woman and her baby. I hope we'll be here tomorrow for dinner. Your uncle can update you then. Right now, I'm taking this to the station, then going back to your uncle's place to work on my book. I'm almost finished now. It needs a deep edit but thank you for opening your retreat to me again while I was here. Who won Word King? Deek?"

"Deek came in second, but we're giving him a consolation prize. It was Piper who took first and is our Word Queen." Cat glanced into the living room as they walked back to the front door. The group was sprawled out on the couches, talking and laughing. Another successful writers' retreat in the books. She laughed as they moved to the front door.

"What's so funny?" Shirley bundled back into her coat and snow boots, watching Cat with curiosity.

"I've just classified a retreat with only one murder as a success." Cat stared out the window at the gently falling snow. It wasn't supposed to snow much tonight and stop in a few hours. Hopefully Seth's drive to Denver and back would be safe tomorrow.

"I think you've just lowered your expectations," Shirley gave her a hug. "Which around here might be a good thing. I know Aspen Hills is a little different, with Covington here and affecting everyone's live, but you have to realize that it can affect even people not attached to the college. Violence just hangs on some people. Even if they aren't the ones to pull the trigger."

"Aspen Hills isn't that bad of a place. I grew up here. I always felt safe." Cat wondered if Shirley had an ulterior motive to point out Aspen Hill's flaws. "Bears live in the forest around here, but I still hike."

Shirley smiled. "Now you sound like your uncle. Anyway, I hope to see you tomorrow for dinner."

And with that, Shirley went outside to a rental she'd gotten at the airport. The first edition *Alice* was tucked under her arm.

Cat left the writers to their own discussion and went into the kitchen where Shauna was reading with a cup of tea. "Can I get one of those?"

"Of course," Shauna responded, closing the book. "The kettle's still hot."

Cat fixed her tea and then sat down at the table. "Shirley just left. She insinuated that Aspen Hills isn't safe and we'll continue to have these murders around the retreat. Do you think she's right?"

Shauna moved the book into the middle of the table and brought her teacup closer. "I don't think there's anywhere that's always safe. Aspen Hills has its share of issues, just like Los Angeles or New York for that matter. I think because we're so small when something like Jewel's death happens, it affects all of us. If we lived in a bigger city, we wouldn't know the person who was killed across town. Shirley's pushing for something else."

"Yeah, I got that idea too. She wants Uncle Pete to move to Alaska. And us too." Cat glanced out the window, but the snow had already stopped. "I don't think I could do Alaska."

"I know I couldn't. Besides, we have the house here. You have connections with the college, good or bad, we're part of this community. And if we want to head south for a week, the airport's two hours away." Shauna sipped her tea. "I know I said we'd talk tomorrow, but I made us reservations in St. Croix. Sun, beach, and a cooking class with the resort's chef. A week of hot days and warm nights. And Andi's agreed to be our house sitter and feed Snow and the Dwarves."

"You think of everything." Cat sipped her tea. "I'm just glad this Jewel thing is settled before Linda has to go back home. She needs to catch a break sometime."

THE NEXT MORNING, the group including Shauna and Seth were in the dining room, talking about the trip back home and the retreat. Cat cut into her waffle and swiped it with butter and hot maple syrup before popping a bite into her mouth. So good.

"I'm going to have to find myself a wife that can cook," Deek said as he got another serving of monkey bread. "Shauna, do you want to move to California and live with me over the bookstore?"

"As enticing as that sounds, I like living in Colorado. Besides, what would I do with Snow? I don't think she'd go up the stairs well." Shauna smiled at Deek. "I've done my time in California. All the traffic and people, Aspen Hills fits my personality better."

"But we do have beaches and great weather," Deek pointed out. "It was worth a try anyway."

"Dude, she's way out of your league," Felix slapped Deek on the back. "Shauna, if I wasn't in a long-term relationship, I'd invite you to Wisconsin."

"Another hard pass," Shauna said laughing. "I haven't had to turn down this many fake proposals since I bartended before moving here. Everyone wanted to whisk me away, like I was some California Barbie Cinderella. And barring that, they'd at least offer a one-night stand. Which I'm not that type of girl at all."

"Bart wanted to marry you and set you up in his Malibu mansion, remember?" Cat had met Shauna in that bar. She'd come in after class to sit and grade papers from her English class at the college a few miles away. Cat lived in walking distance from the bar, so when she wanted company, she headed there to work. And it allowed her to keep her apartment for her fiction writing. Keeping that barrier allowed her to keep her muse from being confused.

"Bart was a lovely man. We just didn't have the spark." Shauna stood and refilled her coffee. "So how was the retreat? Anything we could do differently?"

"Feed us three times a day? But then I'd have to be wheeled out of here." Ryan patted his stomach. "I thought the college dining room was amazing. You're ruining me from ever eating again."

"The retreat was lovely. The accommodations upscale. And the food was amazing." Linda Cook smiled at Shauna and Cat. "You've made this retreat top notch and you even provide emotional support when one of your guests falls apart at a moment's notice."

"It was really great getting to see you, Linda." Cat hoped the retreat hadn't been too hard on her. But she was still standing, which is always a good sigh of emotional toughness.

"And you, Cat. I know we've talked a lot on line, but there's no replacement for face to face interaction." Linda pushed her plate away and took a sip of her coffee. "Sorry about all the murder investigation part of the week. You need to get a break too."

"Believe me, we've got that under control." She met Seth's gaze and they both smiled.

"Oh, so you're just waiting to kick us out of here," Piper teased. "I see you two, I know the score."

"On that note, please have your suitcases downstairs promptly at nine so I can get them tucked away in the van. And if you need to print out a boarding pass..."

"You're an old fart?" Wilder suggested.

"I was going to say, there's a computer and printer in the den on this floor." Seth rolled his eyes. "I can tell the drive to Denver's going to be quiet. Not."

"Not on your life, dude. We're going to raise a fuss until we hit

TSA. Then we'll act like good little girls and boys." Wilder glanced around the room. "Right guys?"

"We didn't agree to this, this was your plan." Piper stood and put her plate in a plastic bin. "Don't get me involved in your Tomfoolery."

"And with that, I'm betting you need to print your boarding pass." Wilder ducked as Piper threw a piece of toast at him. "Thanks. How did you know I wanted more toast?"

Cat met Seth's gaze. "I'm just glad it's you driving them to the airport and not me. I don't think I have the energy to deal with rowdy writers today."

"Aww, Cat, we'd be good if you came with us," Felix elbowed Wilder. "Right?"

"And I'd be giving up four hours of quiet to write." She sipped her coffee. "I love you all, but it's time for you to leave and me to go back to my hermit ways."

"Seth are you sure Cat's not a robot that you guys just turn on during retreat weeks?" Deek winked at Cat as he stood. "No matter. I'll be back soon. I'm enjoying the break from California."

"I'm sure hanging out at the beach and surfing year-round is really hard, not." Wilder stood and followed Deek out of the dining room.

Soon it was just Cat and Linda. She went to refill her coffee, then sat next to Cat. "I wanted to thank you for believing in me. I know I looked like the perfect suspect for your uncle."

"Uncle Pete doesn't look for the perfect suspect, he looks for the right one. I knew you couldn't have killed Jewel, even in a fit of rage." Cat rubbed the top of her coffee cup. "What I don't understand is how Boyd fooled you. You were thinking you saw Tom. Twice."

"With Jewel's announcement, I've been a little on edge. But that bothered me too. I've met Boyd a few times, he is the black sheep of the family, so we didn't hang out at family events much. But I called his Carol and asked her about him. She said he'd lost a lot of weight and had started dying his hair a few months before Tom died. She thought he was going through a midlife crisis. Maybe jealous because he was a high school teacher and Tom was a famous author." Linda paused and sipped her coffee. "Tom wasn't like that though. He wanted a relationship with his brother, but Boyd, he always made excuses. He didn't even come to Tom's memorial service now that I think of it."

"So he told Jewel he was Tom and that's who she was seeing. Then, he told her a bigger lie about him faking his death." Cat thought about the limited times she'd talked to Jewel. "She said she had someone who wanted to buy the book. I wonder if she'd told him about the baby or the book she was writing."

"If she threatened to expose his faked death, it might have pushed Boyd to the edge. He might have been able to explain having an affair and a baby, but taking on Tom's persona? He would have lost both Carol and Jewel." Linda closed her eyes. "At least I wasn't going crazy. I was worried there for a while. You know when you spend a lot of time alone, your mind can play tricks on you."

"I'm sure Tom is watching out for you." Cat glanced at her watch. "And Seth's going to be down here in a few minutes. Do you need help with your luggage?"

SIXTEEN

U ncle Pete pushed back from the table and picked up his plate. "Great dinner as always, Shauna. The ham was perfect."

"I wanted to do something special since Shirley wasn't here for the holidays." Shauna took the plate from him. "Sit down. I've got apple pie for dessert. Cheddar cheese or whipped cream?"

"I'll take the cheese. And thank you." Uncle Pete sat back down. "I am going to have to go in early tomorrow and finish the paperwork on Boyd Cook. The man has issues, that's clear. We're bringing down a specialist from Denver to talk to him tomorrow before we decide the exact charges."

"He's still claiming to be Tom?" Shirley added another serving of scalloped potatoes to her plate. She glanced at Shauna. "The food is amazing, thank you. You didn't have to go to all this trouble for me, especially after just finishing up a retreat week."

"I love to cook, you know that." Shauna beamed at the compliment.

"He's convinced he's his brother, even though his dark hair roots are showing through. He says he didn't even know Jewel." Uncle Pete took the pie and fork that Shauna handed him. "The good news is his prints are all over that cabin. And they're the only ones on the fireplace poker. So we know he killed her. And we have her phone with messages from both of them. Along with a hotel manager in New Jersey that says that Boyd and Jewel were regular customers. And, although he made the reservations in Tom Cook's name, the credit card he used said Boyd. The manager said his clerk had him approve it since Boyd said Tom was his pen name."

"He went completely down the rabbit hole," Seth commented. "In for a penny, my mom used to say."

"Which is why the need for a specialist before we do any charging. I don't want him walking free based on a technicality. I'd be worried for Linda Cook's safety. How is she doing?" Uncle Pete didn't look up when he asked the question, but Cat knew it was aimed at her.

"She called when she got home, thanked me for the retreat, again. And said she was going to get an appointment with a grief counselor. She hadn't done it earlier and now she thinks it's time for her to move on." Cat smiled as she took a last bite of ham. "She finished her book about life with Tom. She's doing one last run for edits, then she's going to start shopping for an agent. I gave her my agent's name and told her to use me as a reference. So fingers crossed."

"I hope I can count on your help too," Shirley stood and took her plate to the sink. "I'll be ready to shop this book next month. I think. I've never been so nervous in my life. I wasn't this nervous when I was hunting a serial killer."

Shauna pointed to the plates with pie on the counter. "I have whipped cream in the dispenser there. Or do you want cheese like Pete?"

"I'm a whipped cream, girl, thank you." As Shirley brought back her dessert, Cat started to stand.

Shauna waved her off. "I'll get it."

"Thanks. And Shirley, of course, I'll send you my agent's name and email. The retreat might just become a good source of clients for her." Cat took the pie from Shauna. "I shouldn't eat this since we're going to be on the beach in less than a week."

"And eating while we're there. This resort is known for more than just a beautiful beach. It's run by a famous chef that left the bustle of owning several restaurants all over the country. He's writing a cookbook now." Shauna switched out her plate for pie. "I'm so excited to work next to him in his kitchen for a week."

"We don't have to cook for our supper, right?" Seth stood and switched out his plate for pie as well. He drowned the slice in a lot of whipped cream.

"No, cooking with him was an upgrade I only bought for me." Shauna's eyes glowed with the pleasure of cooking with a real chef.

"I would think if you were working, that your cost should be less." Uncle Pete shook his head as he looked around the table. "Am I missing something?"

ACKNOWLEDGMENTS

Cat Latimer and her friends was the second series I wrote and the first where I was trying to expand into a new format (mass market paperback.) I came up with the original idea of a writer getting the old house she loved (and lost in the divorce) back when her ex-husband died during a road trip to Idaho. I was also looking into attending a retreat at the time so it made sense to build my own. I still haven't gone on a formal retreat, but I've made my own in my personal life as well. Now that the success or failure of the series is back in my own hands, I've been grateful for all the readers who still love Cat, Shauna, and Seth, and want to know what's next. So keep the messages and letters coming.

OTHER CAT LATIMER MYSTERIES

LEGAL BITS

Murder on a Snowy Evening: A Cat Latimer Mystery by Lynn Cahoon

Published by Lynn Cahoon
www.lynncahoon.com
Copyright © 2023 Lynn Cahoon

Cover by Earthly Charms

Printed in Great Britain
by Amazon